HATCHET

Gary Paulsen

WITH RELATED READINGS

THE EMC MASTERPIECE SERIES

Access Editions

EMC/Paradigm Publishing

St. Paul, Minnesota

Staff Credits

Laurie Skiba
Editorial Content Director

Brenda Owens
Senior Editor

Jennifer J. Anderson
Associate Editor

Nichola Torbett
Associate Editor

Chris Lee
Associate Editor

Keri Henkel
Assistant Editor

Ashley Kuehl
Assistant Editor

Sara Hyry
Becky Palmer
Contributing Writers

Paul Spencer
Art and Photo Researcher

Valerie Murphy
Editorial Assistant

Shelley Clubb
Production Manager

Lisa Beller
Design and Production Specialist

Petrina Nyhan
Production Specialist

Leslie Anderson
Cover Designer

Parkwood Composition
Compositor

Cheryl Drivdahl
Proofreader

The edition is reprinted by arrangement with Simon & Schuster Books For Young Readers, Simon & Schuster Children's Publishing Division. Copyright © 1987 by Gary Paulsen. All rights reserved.

Cover image © Tim Thompson / Corbis

Author photo © Ruth Wright Paulsen

Library of Congress Cataloging-in-Publication Data

Paulsen, Gary.
  Hatchet : with related readings / Gary Paulsen.
  p. cm. – (The EMC masterpiece series access editions)
  Includes plot analysis, related readings, activities, and projects.
  Sequel: The river.
  Newbery Honor Book, 1988
  Summary: After a plane crash, thirteen-year-old Brian spends fifty-four days in the Canadian wilderness, learning to survive with only the aid of a hatchet given him by his mother, and learning also to survive his parents' divorce.
  ISBN 0-8219-2960-7
  [1. Survival—Fiction. 2. Divorce—Fiction. 3. Canada—Fiction.] I. Title. II. Series.

  PZ7.P2843Hat2004
  [Fic]—dc22

                                                            2004061990

ISBN 0-8219-2960-7
Copyright © 2005 by EMC Corporation

Published by EMC/Paradigm Publishing
875 Montreal Way
St. Paul, Minnesota 55102
800-328-1452
www.emcp.com
E-mail: educate@emcp.com

Printed in the United States of America.
  2 3 4 5 6 7 8 9 10 xxx 11 10 09 08

Table of Contents

THE LIFE AND WORKS OF

Gary Paulsen

Gary Paulsen (1939–) is one of the most popular writers for young people today. He has written nearly 200 books, hundreds of articles and short stories, and several plays. Many of Paulsen's stories draw upon his own experiences, which include such adventures as racing sled dogs, working as an ambulance driver, and riding a motorcycle from New Mexico to Alaska.

Gary Paulsen

Gary Paulsen was born in 1939 in Minneapolis, Minnesota. He had a difficult childhood. When he was born, his father was in Europe fighting in World War II, and his mother had to work in a factory to support her young son. Paulsen's grandmother and aunts helped to raise him during his early years.

In 1946, Paulsen and his mother joined his father who was then stationed at an army base in the Philippines. During their boat voyage across the Pacific, they saw a plane that was forced to make an emergency landing on the ocean. Paulsen watched as sharks killed crash survivors trying to swim to rescue boats. The memory of this tragedy stuck with him, and would later help inspire him to write about the plane crash in *Hatchet*.

The Paulsen family returned to the United States in 1949, but continued to move frequently from one army base to another. Paulsen's home life was unstable, not only because of the frequent moving, but also because his parents were alcoholics and often abusive. Gary ran away from home several times and went to stay with relatives. Once, when he was 14, he ran away and joined a traveling carnival.

One day, something happened that changed Gary's life. While out delivering newspapers in the below-zero temperatures of his northern Minnesota town, he took shelter from the cold in a public library. To his surprise, the librarian offered him a book and a library card. As Paulsen tells it, "The librarian kept giving me things to take home and read—westerns, science fiction, and every once in a while a classic. . . . When she handed me a library card, she handed me the world. I roared through everything she gave me. It was as though I had been dying of thirst and the librarian had handed me a five-gallon bucket of water." Today, Paulsen believes that reading is the most important training for writers.

Still, Gary did not begin to write books right away. In 1957–1958, he worked as a trapper in order to pay his tuition at Bemidji College (now Bemidji State University) in Minnesota, then joined the army. He took courses and became a field engineer from 1962 to 1966. Then he went to California to become a magazine proofreader. While working at that job, he began writing on his first book, *Special War*. This nonfiction work for adults was published in 1966, when Paulsen was 27. After that, he was off and running. Paulsen published about 40 books and many short stories and articles during the early years of his career.

Then, in 1977, Paulsen was sued for libel over his novel *Winterkill*, by some people who thought they recognized themselves in the book. Paulsen won the lawsuit, but it left him bankrupt and unhappy about writing. He stopped writing for a while. To support his family, he trapped beavers. Somebody gave him a dog team to help him expand his trapping efforts. This inspired Paulsen to enter the Iditarod, a dogsled race in Alaska. A publisher sponsored his first run. Paulsen's interest in dogsledding shows up in his writing, in books such as *Dogsong* and *Woodsong*. While training his dog team, Paulsen did a lot of writing during the dogs' rest periods.

When a heart condition forced Paulsen to stop racing, he turned the time he spent training his dogs to writing. That gave him 18–20 hours a day to devote to writing! Since then, he has written many popular books, such as *Hatchet, The River, Nightjohn,* and *Brian's Winter*. Paulsen writes, on average, more than a book a year.

Paulsen's books are favorites among young people. He wrote *Brian's Winter* in response to the hundreds of letters he received from readers who asked "what if" questions about Brian's experience in *Hatchet.* Paulsen's works also are well received by critics, teachers, and librarians. Three of Paulsen's books were named Newbery Honor Books: *Hatchet, Dogsong,* and *The Winter Room.* He has won many other awards for his books as well.

Today, Gary Paulsen lives in New Mexico with his wife, Ruth Wright Paulsen, an artist who has illustrated several of his books. They spend a good deal of their time on a boat in the Pacific. He continues to write stories for young people.

Selected Fiction for Young People by Gary Paulsen

Here are just a few more of the many books Gary Paulsen has written for young people. Check them out!

Dogsong (1986)
Seeking to escape modern ways, a 14-year-old Eskimo boy takes a dog team and sled on a dangerous 1400-mile journey across the Alaskan tundra. This book won a Newbery Honor.

The Winter Room (1989)
Two boys growing up on a farm spend the winter listening to their great-uncle David's amazing stories about his life as a lumberjack in the north woods. Then one night Uncle David tells the story, "The Woodcutter," and what happens next is terrible—then wonderful. This book won a Newbery Honor.

Nightjohn (1993)
A historical novel about a slave who teaches other slaves how to read. This was also made into a movie on the Disney Channel.

More books about Brian:
The River (1991)
Brian is asked to return to the wilderness two years after the events in *Hatchet,* so the astronauts and the military can learn the survival techniques that kept him alive. But no sooner does he arrive there than something goes dreadfully wrong.

Brian's Winter (1996)
What if Brian had not been rescued, and had to survive the long, cold winter in the Canadian wilderness? This book was written to answer that question!

Brian's Return (1999)
After his experiences in *Hatchet*, Brian can no longer fit into his old life—nothing makes sense to him anymore. He finally decides he must return to the wilderness again, this time, perhaps never to return.

Brian's Hunt (2003)
Brian is at home in the Canadian wilderness and has even made friends. Then one day he comes across a dog who has been terribly wounded. He must hunt out the cause.

Selected Nonfiction for Young People by Gary Paulsen

Here are some nonfiction works by Gary Paulsen that explore the theme of survival.

Father Water, Mother Woods (1994)
A book of essays about Paulsen's experiences hunting, fishing, and camping in the wilderness.

Guts: The True Stories Behind Hatchet *and the Brian Books* (2001)
A collection of stories about the real-life experiences that inspired Paulsen's books.

Woodsong (2002)
An autobiographical book about Paulsen's experiences dogsledding, including an exciting account of his first Iditarod sled race.

My Life in Dog Years (1998)
Puppies, Dogs, and Blue Northers: Reflections on Being Raised by a Pack of Sled Dogs (1998)
These books are filled with funny anecdotes and great description about Paulsen's experiences with dogs, particularly sled dogs. The second book tells about how he raised a litter of sled dogs.

Time Line of Gary Paulsen's Life

Paulsen is born on May 17 in Minneapolis, Minnesota.	1939
Paulsen moves with his family to an Army base in the Philippines where his father is stationed.	1946
Paulsen and his family return to the United States.	1949
Paulsen leaves home at the age of fourteen to join a traveling carnival.	1953
Paulsen attends Bemidji College in Bemidji, Minnesota.	1957–1958
Paulsen serves in the U.S. Army.	1959–1962
Paulsen's first book, a nonfiction work for adults, is published.	1966
Paulsen attends the University of Colorado.	1972
Paulsen publishes *Winterkill* and fights a lawsuit over the book.	1977
Paulsen enters his first Iditarod, a dogsled race in Alaska.	1983
Paulsen enters the Iditarod for the second time. He has heart problems and gives up dog racing. *Dogsong* is published and named a Newbery Honor Book.	1985
Hatchet is published.	1981
Hatchet is named an American Library Association Notable Best Book.	1987
Hatchet is named a Newbery Honor Book and earns a *Booklist* Editor's Choice citation.	1988
The Winter Room is published.	1989
The Winter Room is named a Newbery Honor Book.	1990
The River is published.	1991
Brian's Winter is published.	1996
Brian's Return is published.	1999
Guts is published.	2001
Brian's Hunt is published.	2003

Context for *Hatchet*

At the beginning of *Hatchet,* Brian Robeson, the main character, is on a small plane flying from Hampton, New York, to the oilfields of Canada. After the plane crashes, Brian must find a way to survive alone in the Canadian wilderness. To understand Brian's experience, you should know a little about the setting of the book, what small planes are like, and some information about survival and rescue technology.

Canadian Forests

The site of Brian's plane crash is probably somewhere in Ontario or Quebec. These provinces are part of the Canadian Shield, a region that covers about half of Canada in a horseshoe shape. Thousands of years ago, glaciers passed through this area and formed its characteristically rugged landscape, leaving a rocky terrain, small hills, and many lakes. In the Canadian shield, the summers are short and cool, and winters are very long and cold.

The forests of the Canadian Shield are made up of both evergreen and deciduous trees, including white and black spruce, white birch, fir, white and red pine, sugar maple, red maple, eastern hemlock, red oak, and white ash. The area is also home to berry bushes, fruit trees, and nut bushes, as Brian finds out in the book.

Many animals make their home in the Canadian forests. Some of the animals that Brian encounters in the book are moose, black bears, rabbits, wolves, porcupines, turtles, and skunks. In addition, he sees ruffed grouse (also called partridges, ruffled grouse, or drummers) and is plagued by mosquitos, which in spring and summer are quite thick in the north woods.

Moose are large animals. They can be as tall as 6.5 feet at the shoulder and weigh over a thousand pounds. The males have large antlers. Moose like to live near water. They eat grass, other plants, and bark. Moose are considered unpredictable animals and are known to attack humans without warning.

Black bears are omnivores, meaning they eat both plants and animals. Mostly, they eat fruit, nuts, and green plants. Black bears usually do not attack people. However, as people take over more and more of the black bears' habitat, there are more and more bear-people interactions, which can lead to some attacks. Also, bears can smell food and other scented items, like soap and sunscreen. They often try to get at whatever they smell. For example, bears may try to get into a backpack or tent if they smell food. People who are camping should keep food hung away from their sleeping area or use special bear boxes.

Porcupines and skunks have unique ways of protecting themselves. Porcupines can hit enemies with their quill-covered tails, leaving quills stuck in the victim's skin. The barbed quills are difficult and painful to remove. Skunks protect themselves by means of a noxious fluid which they spray from glands under their tails. This "musk" smells terrible and is so strong it can burn the eyes and nose and cause temporary blindness.

Ruffed grouse live in areas from northern Canada to Georgia. The northern birds are grayish brown with dark feathers on their neck. Ruffed grouse use their coloring and an ability to stay quite still to avoid being caught by predators. If startled, they rise up in a loud flurry of activity.

In the Canadian forest, insects including mosquitos and black flies can be numerous in spring and summer. They swarm around and bite humans and other animals. These insects can make it extremely uncomfortable for people to spend time outdoors during certain times of the year.

Bush Planes

In remote areas, such as the remote region of Canada to which Brian travels in *Hatchet*, bush planes are the best, and sometimes only, way to get from place to place. Bush planes are small, rugged planes used to carry people, supplies, and other materials. In addition to wheels, many bush planes have floats for landing on lakes. Others have skis for winter landings. Bush planes need less space to take off and land than larger passenger planes do. They also fly lower than larger planes.

It takes special training to fly small planes. The autopilot mechanism may help a pilot keep on the right course, but it takes knowledge and experience to handle take-offs, landings, and problems. One thing pilots need to know how to do is to make an emergency landing in case of engine failure. In emergency landing, the pilot must aim the plane in the direction of an open area, such as a field or lake. He or she tries to avoid making turns because they take a lot of energy—energy that is needed to keep the plane going fast enough to reach the landing spot.

Bush pilots are required to file their flight plans with an airport or aviation control agency, and can connect by radio to the nearest aviation control tower if they have problems. According to Canadian air regulations, pilots must supposed to carry what they need to make a fire, create shelter, purify water, and signal distress. Wilderness pilots also are encouraged to pack food, cooking utensils, a compass, an axe, a saw, fishing equipment, mosquito netting and insect repellent, winter sleeping bags, snowshoes (for winter or areas where snow is likely), a sharp knife, and a survival manual.

Survival Skills

People who are stranded in the wilderness, in the arctic, in a desert, or at sea need similar survival skills. They all need to protect themselves from the weather and animals, get water and food, and try to signal for help. How they go about doing these things will vary based on their environment. For example, a person lost in a forested area would have very different options for food than a person stranded in the desert. The following tips can help a person survive in a forested wilderness such as the one Brian's plane crashes into in the book.

Be prepared. The first rule of survival in the wilderness is to be prepared. That means being dressed appropriately, carrying enough food and water, having and knowing how to use a map and compass, and packing other gear that may help you stay alive or get rescued if something goes wrong.

Be mentally prepared. If you get lost, hurt, or stranded for some other reason, stay calm. Panicking doesn't help. In order to take care of yourself, you need to stay focused and think clearly. Hope is important. Think about people looking for you. Picture yourself getting out of the situation. Then do things that keep you alive, that help you escape, or that help others find you.

Assess your options. Whether you try to walk out of the woods or stay put and hope to be rescued will depend on several factors. Generally if you are lost, it is a good idea to stay put. If you know where you are and have a compass and map, you may want to try to hike out during daylight. You should know how to use the compass and map and that you have what you need to walk for as long as it will take you. Remember, you will need more energy to walk out of the woods than to stay put, especially if the terrain is rugged. Staying put is usually the best option and may provide the best chance of rescue. When you stay put, you will need to take care of some basic needs.

Make a shelter. One of the first things you should do if you realize you are stranded is to build a shelter. A good shelter will protect you from sun, rain, snow, and wind. Staying dry is important because if you get wet, you may get cold and develop hypothermia, a dangerous condition in which your body loses too much heat.

Fallen trees, caves, and other natural objects can form partial shelters. You can add tree branches or other materials to make your shelter more protective. If possible, choose an area near water, food, and fuel. Be careful when building a shelter near ditches or water, though—these areas could flood. A garbage bag, poncho, or waterproof jacket, can help keep you warm and dry. If it is cool, a hood or hat can offer additional protection.

Find safe water. Humans can survive only a few days without water. Dehydration makes it harder for you to stay warm. It can also make it harder for you to think clearly. When hiking in the woods, you should always carry water with you. It is also a good idea to have a water filter or treatment system. This will help you avoid diseases that pass through water. Boiling your water also may make it safer to drink.

If you are stranded, you may need to drink untreated water. You can find water in lakes or streams. You also may find water trapped on leaf tops or get water from eating the stems and leaves of plants. If you have a pan and a fire or stove, snow and ice can be melted to create drinkable water. Trying to melt ice or snow in your mouth may lead to hypothermia.

Make a fire. Fire serves many purposes if you are lost in the woods. Most importantly, it warms you and helps dry your clothes. It also provides a way to cook food or boil water. A fire also can keep away bugs and some animals. Finally, a fire allows you to signal for help.

When building a fire, choose the spot carefully so that you don't start a forest fire. Gather the materials to build a fire. You will need tinder, kindling, and logs for fuel. Pile the materials loosely to allow plenty of air into your fire. If you have a matches or a lighter, it will be easy to light your fire. If not, use glass and sunlight to start the fire or flint (a kind of rock) and steel. A fire may be difficult to start if you don't have matches or a lighter, so try to keep the fire going once it is started.

Find food. Unless you are found quickly, you will probably need to eat while you are stranded. If you have food with you, you can eat that first. Remember, food gives you the strength you need to do other things.

If you need to find food in the wild, be careful to avoid poisonous plants. Here are some general tips to do that:

- Avoid green and white berries, as they are poisonous. About half of the red berries are poisonous.
- Avoid bitter-tasting plants.

- Avoid plants that smell like almonds.
- Avoid eating mushrooms. They could be very poisonous.
- Avoid eating any plant parts that are rotting or show signs of mold.

If possible, choose plants you know are safe to eat. Even plants that are not poisonous may cause sickness if you eat too much. Eat small portions of wild foods.

Rescue Technology

Cell phones are becoming the most widely used means of calling for help from remote areas. Cell phones, however, are useless if the battery is dead or there is no signal in the area. Some people think carrying a cell phone is being prepared, but there is no guarantee that you will be able to make a call if you need to.

Personal locator beacons (PLB) are small beacons that transmit a signal for about 24 hours. These beacons transmit a signal through satellites to help search and rescue teams find a lost person.

In the book, Brian has no cell phone or PLB. Instead, he must rely on low-tech means of getting help. There are many simple ways to create a signal of distress or draw attention to yourself. You can build a signal fire; just be careful not to start the forest on fire. Mirrors or other shiny things that reflect light can help people notice you. Flares, flags, or whistles will attract attention. You can also make ground signals out of branches, logs, rocks, or other objects. To be seen from above, ground signals should be about 30 feet long and 9 feet wide.

Characters in
Hatchet

Main Character

Brian Robeson. Brian Robeson is a thirteen-year-old boy. At the beginning of the book, he is on his way to visit his father in Canada. His parents have recently been divorced, and he is upset about the Secret he knows about his mother. After his plane crashes in the Canadian wilderness, Brian must deal with much deeper worries—he must figure out how to stay alive. In his struggle to survive and overcome hardship, Brian grows and changes in ways he never thought possible.

Minor Characters

Mrs. Robeson. In a flashback at the beginning of the story, we learn that Brian's mother drove him to the airport and gave him the hatchet. We learn more about her throughout the story through Brian's thoughts and memories.

The Pilot. The pilot of Brian's bush plane is a man in his mid-forties. Brian doesn't remember his name, but thinks it's Jake or Jim.

Terry. Terry is Brian's friend. Like Brian's mother, Terry appears in Brian's thoughts and dreams.

Mr. Robeson. Brian's father is a mechanical engineer who designed and invented a new drill bit for oil drilling. He is working in the oil fields of Canada, which is where Brian is supposed to stay with him for the summer. We learn about Brian's father through Brian's thoughts and dreams.

Echoes

Quotations On Survival

"Man can live about forty days without food, about three days without water, about eight minutes without air, but only for one second without hope."

—Anonymous

"It is not the strongest of the species that survives, nor the most intelligent that survives. It is the one that is the most adaptable to change."
—Charles Darwin

"Hunger, love, pain, and fear are some of those inner forces which rule the individual's instinct for self preservation."

—Albert Einstein

From Gary Paulsen

"Fall came on with a softness, so that Brian didn't realize what was in store—a hard-spined north woods winter—until it was nearly too late."
—from *Brian's Winter*

"The hawk did not hunt to kill. It hunted to eat. Of course it had to kill to eat—along with all other carnivorous animals—but the killing was the means to bring food, not the end. Only man hunted for sport, or for trophies.
  It is the same with me as with the hawk."

—from *Brian's Return*

"Maybe I didn't understand what you said—let me get it straight. You want me to go back and do it over again? Live in the woods with nothing but a hatchet?"

—from *The River*

"He was in his world again. He was back.
  It was high summer coming to fall and Brian was back in the far reaches of wilderness—or as he thought of it now, home."

—from *Brian's Hunt*

"So much of what I did as a boy came to be part of Brian—all of it, in some ways. I hope that *Guts* satisfies those readers who want to know more about Brian and my life."
—from *Guts: The True Stories Behind* Hatchet *and the Brian Books*

Images of the Canadian Wilderness

Photo © Charles Krebs/CORBIS

The Canadian Shield area around Hudson Bay covers about half of Canada in a horse-shoe shape. The region is covered with rocks, hills, lakes, and forests. The forests, a mix of evergreen and deciduous trees, are home to many animals.

Black bears have a keen sense of smell and hearing, but they have poor eyesight. They are omnivores, meaning they eat both plants and animals. They are most active before sunrise and after sunset. They usually do not attack people. If provoked, however, they use their claws and teeth to defend themselves.

Photo © Lynda Richardson/CORBIS

Snapping turtles are found in shallow areas near lakes, rivers, and streams. In water, they are shy and swim away from intruders. On land, they bite, or snap at, possible attackers. In late June or July, female snapping turtles lay between 20 and 80 eggs in earthen nests. The eggs, which are round and white, are the size of ping pong balls. The eggs hatch in September or early October.

Critical Viewing Question
These photographs show images of plant and animal life in the Canadian wilderness. How are these images the same as or different from images in your surroundings?

Photo © W. Perry/CORBIS

Skunks have a unique way of protecting themselves. When threatened, skunks spray a noxious fluid. This spray smells terrible and can cause pain and temporary blindness.

Moose like to live near water. They eat grass, other plants, and bark. They are considered unpredictable and may attack humans without warning.

Map of Canada

This map of Canada includes all of the provinces of the Canadian Shield, the rocky, forested area that surrounds Hudson Bay. Which provinces border Hudson Bay? Why might bush planes be the most common method of transportation in many areas of the Shield?

Chapter 1

Brian Robeson stared out the window of the small plane at the endless green northern wilderness below. It was a small plane, a Cessna 406—a bushplane—and the engine was so loud, so roaring and <u>consuming</u> and loud, that it ruined any chance for conversation.

Not that he had much to say. He was thirteen and the only passenger on the plane with a pilot named—what was it? Jim or Jake or something—who was in his mid-forties and who had been silent as he worked to prepare for take-off. In fact since Brian had come to the small airport in Hampton, New York to meet the plane—driven by his mother—the pilot had spoken only five words to him.

"Get in the copilot's seat."

Which Brian had done. They had taken off and that was the last of the conversation. There had been the <u>initial</u> excitement, of course. He had never flown in a single-engine plane before and to be sitting in the copilot's seat with all the controls right there in front of him, all the instruments in his face as the plane clawed for altitude, jerking and sliding on the wind currents as the pilot took off, had been interesting and exciting. But in five minutes they had

◀ *Why was Brian excited at first?*

| words for everyday use | **con • sum • ing** (kən sü′ miŋ) *adj.*, engrossing, taking all attention. *Joy eats, sleeps, and dreams hockey; it's her* <u>consuming</u> *passion.* | **ini • tial** (in ish′ əl) *adj.*, first. *After my* <u>initial</u> *fear, I enjoyed the ride.* |

leveled off at six thousand feet and headed northwest and from then on the pilot had been silent, staring out the front, and the <u>drone</u> of the engine had been all that was left. The drone and the sea of green trees that lay before the plane's nose and flowed to the horizon, spread with lakes, swamps, and wandering streams and rivers.

Now Brian sat, looking out the window with the roar thundering through his ears, and tried to catalog what had led up to his taking this flight.

The thinking started.

Always it started with a single word.

Divorce.

▶ How does Brian feel about his parents' divorce?

It was an ugly word, he thought. A tearing, ugly word that meant fights and yelling, lawyers—God, he thought, how he hated lawyers who sat with their comfortable smiles and tried to explain to him in legal terms how all that he lived in was coming apart—and the breaking and shattering of all the solid things. His home, his life—all the solid things. Divorce. A breaking word, an ugly breaking word.

Divorce.

Secrets.

▶ What does Brian think about a lot?

No, not secrets so much as just the Secret. What he knew and had not told anybody, what he knew about his mother that had caused the divorce, what he knew, what he knew—the Secret.

Divorce.

The Secret.

Brian felt his eyes beginning to burn and knew there would be tears. He had cried for a time, but that was gone now. He didn't cry now. Instead his eyes burned and tears came, the seeping tears that burned, but he didn't cry. He wiped his eyes with a finger and looked at the pilot out of the corner of his eye to make sure he hadn't noticed the burning and tears.

---

words for everyday use   **drone** (drōn) *n.*, continuous deep buzzing or humming sound. *The <u>drone</u> of the bees is a constant sound in the garden.*

The pilot sat large, his hands lightly on the wheel, feet on the rudder[1] pedals. He seemed more a machine than a man, an extension of the plane. On the dashboard in front of him Brian saw dials, switches, meters, knobs, levers, cranks, lights, handles that were wiggling and flickering, all indicating nothing that he understood and the pilot seemed the same way. Part of the plane, not human.

When he saw Brian look at him, the pilot seemed to open up a bit and he smiled. "Ever fly in the copilot's seat before?" He leaned over and lifted the headset off his right ear and put it on his temple, yelling to overcome the sound of the engine.

Brian shook his head. He had never been in any kind of plane, never seen the cockpit of a plane except in films or on television. It was loud and confusing. "First time."

"It's not as complicated as it looks. Good plane like this almost flies itself." The pilot shrugged. "Makes my job easy." He took Brian's left arm. "Here, put your hands on the controls, your feet on the rudder pedals, and I'll show you what I mean."

◀ What does the pilot say about flying the plane?

Brian shook his head. "I'd better not."

"Sure. Try it . . ."

Brian reached out and took the wheel in a grip so tight his knuckles were white. He pushed his feet down on the pedals. The plane <u>slewed</u> suddenly to the right.

"Not so hard. Take her light, take her light."

Brian eased off, relaxed his grip. The burning in his eyes was forgotten momentarily as the vibration of the plane came through the wheel and the pedals. It seemed almost alive.

◀ How does the plane seem to Brian when he is flying it?

"See?" The pilot let go of his wheel, raised his hands in the air and took his feet off the pedals to show Brian he was actually flying the plane alone.

---

1. **rudder.** Part of a plane that controls direction

words for everyday use   slew (slü) v., turn suddenly, skid. *The car <u>slewed</u> to the right when we hit the black ice.*

"Simple. Now turn the wheel a little to the right and push on the right rudder pedal a small amount."

Brian turned the wheel slightly and the plane immediately banked[2] to the right, and when he pressed on the right rudder pedal the nose slid across the horizon to the right. He left off on the pressure and straightened the wheel and the plane righted itself.

"Now you can turn. Bring her back to the left a little."

Brian turned the wheel left, pushed on the left pedal, and the plane came back around. "It's easy." He smiled. "At least this part."

The pilot nodded. "All of flying is easy. Just takes learning. Like everything else. Like everything else." He took the controls back, then reached up and rubbed his left shoulder. "Aches and pains—must be getting old."

Brian let go of the controls and moved his feet away from the pedals as the pilot put his hands on the wheel. "Thank you . . ."

But the pilot had put his headset back on and the gratitude was lost in the engine noise and things went back to Brian looking out the window at the ocean of trees and lakes. The burning eyes did not come back, but memories did, came flooding in. The words. Always the words.

Divorce.

The Secret.

Fights.

Split.

The big split. Brian's father did not understand as Brian did, knew only that Brian's mother wanted to break the marriage apart. The split had come and then the divorce, all so fast, and the court had left him with his mother except for the summers and what the judge called "visitation rights." So formal. Brian hated judges as he hated lawyers. Judges that leaned over the bench and asked Brian if he understood where he was to live and why. Judges who did not know what had really happened. Judges with the

---

2. **banked.** Inclined or moved up to the side

caring look that meant nothing as lawyers said legal phrases that meant nothing.

In the summer Brian would live with his father. In the school year with his mother. That's what the judge said after looking at papers on his desk and listening to the lawyers talk. Talk. Words.

Now the plane <u>lurched</u> slightly to the right and Brian looked at the pilot. He was rubbing his shoulder again and there was the sudden smell of body gas in the plane. Brian turned back to avoid embarrassing the pilot, who was obviously in some discomfort. Must have stomach troubles.

So this summer, this first summer when he was allowed to have "visitation rights" with his father, with the divorce only one month old, Brian was heading north. His father was a mechanical engineer who had designed or invented a new drill bit for oil drilling, a self-cleaning, self-sharpening bit. He was working in the oil fields of Canada, up on the tree line where the tundra[3] started and the forests ended. Brian was riding up from New York with some drilling equipment—it was lashed down in the rear of the plane next to a fabric bag the pilot had called a survival pack, which had emergency supplies in case they had to make an emergency landing—that had to be specially made in the city, riding in a bushplane with the pilot named Jim or Jake or something who had turned out to be an all right guy, letting him fly and all.

Except for the smell. Now there was a constant odor, and Brian took another look at the pilot, found him rubbing his shoulder and down the arm now, the left arm, letting go more gas and <u>wincing</u>. Probably something he ate, Brian thought.

His mother had driven him from the city to meet the plane at Hampton where it came to pick up the

◄ Where is Brian going and why?

◄ What is in the back of the plane?

◄ What does Brian notice about the pilot?

---

3. **tundra.** Treeless plain of the arctic and subarctic region

words for everyday use	lurch (lurch) *v.*, roll or tip suddenly. *When the plane <u>lurched</u>, everyone was thrown to the right.* wince (win[t]s) *v.*, to shrink or draw back	slightly, usually with a grimace, as in pain, embarrassment, or alarm. *Darcy <u>winced</u> when her hand brushed the hot pan on the stove.*

drilling equipment. A drive in silence, a long drive in silence. Two and a half hours of sitting in the car, staring out the window just as he was now staring out the window of the plane. Once, after an hour, when they were out of the city she turned to him.

"Look, can't we talk this over? Can't we talk this out? Can't you tell me what's bothering you?"

And there were the words again. Divorce. Split. The Secret. How could he tell her what he knew? So he had remained silent, shook his head and continued to stare unseeing at the countryside, and his mother had gone back to driving only to speak to him one more time when they were close to Hampton.

She reached over the back of the seat and brought up a paper sack. "I got something for you, for the trip."

Brian took the sack and opened the top. Inside there was a hatchet, the kind with a steel handle and a rubber handgrip. The head was in a stout leather case that had a brass-riveted belt loop.

"It goes on your belt." His mother spoke now without looking at him. There were some farm trucks on the road now and she had to weave through them and watch traffic. "The man at the store said you could use it. You know. In the woods with your father."

▶ How does Brian feel about his mother's gift?

Dad, he thought. Not "my father." My dad. "Thanks. It's really nice." But the words sounded hollow, even to Brian.

"Try it on. See how it looks on your belt."

And he would normally have said no, would normally have said no that it looked too <u>hokey</u> to have a hatchet on your belt. Those were the normal things he would say. But her voice was thin, had a sound like something thin that would break if you touched it, and he felt bad for not speaking to her. Knowing what he knew, even with the anger, the hot white

---

words for everyday use

hok • ey (hō′ kē) *adj.,* corny. *Jed thought a campfire singalong was <u>hokey</u>, but his mother said it was tradition.*

hate of his anger at her, he still felt bad for not speaking to her, and so to humor her he loosened his belt and pulled the right side out and put the hatchet on and rethreaded the belt.

"Scootch around so I can see."

He moved around in the seat, feeling only slightly ridiculous.

She nodded. "Just like a scout. My little scout." And there was the tenderness in her voice that she had when he was small, the tenderness that she had when he was small and sick, with a cold, and she put her hand on his forehead, and the burning came into his eyes again and he had turned away from her and looked out the window, forgotten the hatchet on his belt and so arrived at the plane with the hatchet still on his belt.

Because it was a bush flight from a small airport there had been no security and the plane had been waiting, with the engine running when he arrived and he had grabbed his suitcase and pack bag and run for the plane without stopping to remove the hatchet.

So it was still on his belt. At first he had been embarrassed but the pilot had said nothing about it and Brian forgot it as they took off and began flying.

More smell now. Bad. Brian turned again to glance at the pilot, who had both hands on his stomach and was grimacing in pain, reaching for the left shoulder again as Brian watched.

"Don't know, kid . . ." The pilot's words were a hiss, barely <u>audible</u>. "Bad aches here. Bad aches. Thought it was something I ate but . . ."

He stopped as a fresh <u>spasm</u> of pain hit him. Even Brian could see how bad it was—the pain drove the pilot back into the seat, back and down.

"I've never had anything like this . . ."

The pilot reached for the switch on his mike cord, his hand coming up in a small arc from his stomach,

◄ Why didn't Brian remove the hatchet from his belt?

---

words for everyday use

au • di • ble (ôd′ ə bəl) *adj.*, capable of being heard. *The speaker was barely <u>audible</u> over all the construction noise in the street.*

spasm (spaz′ əm) *n.* sudden, involuntary muscle movement. *A <u>spasm</u> of pain shook Ni's whole body.*

and he flipped the switch and said, "This is flight four six . . ."

And now a jolt took him like a hammerblow, so forcefully that he seemed to crush back into the seat, and Brian reached for him, could not understand at first what it was, could not know.

And then knew.

Brian knew. The pilot's mouth went rigid, he swore and jerked a short series of slams into the seat, holding his shoulder now. Swore and hissed, "Chest! Oh God, my chest is coming apart!"

Brian knew now.

▶ What is happening to the pilot?

The pilot was having a heart attack. Brian had been in the shopping mall with his mother when a man in front of Paisley's store had suffered a heart attack. He had gone down and screamed about his chest. An old man. Much older than the pilot.

Brian knew.

The pilot was having a heart attack and even as the knowledge came to Brian he saw the pilot slam into the seat one more time, one more awful time he slammed back into the seat and his right leg jerked, pulling the plane to the side in a sudden twist and his head fell forward and spit came. Spit came from the corners of his mouth and his legs contracted up, up into the seat, and his eyes rolled back in his head until there was only white.

Only white for his eyes and the smell became worse, filled the cockpit, and all of it so fast, so incredibly fast that Brian's mind could not take it in at first. Could only see it in stages.

The pilot had been talking, just a moment ago, complaining of the pain. He had been talking.

Then the jolts had come.

The jolts that took the pilot back had come, and now Brian sat and there was a strange feeling of silence in the thrumming roar of the engine—a strange feeling of silence and being alone. Brian was stopped.

He was stopped. Inside he was stopped. He could not think past what he saw, what he felt. All was stopped. The very core of him, the very center of Brian Robeson was stopped and stricken with a white-flash of horror, a terror so intense that his breathing, his thinking, and nearly his heart had stopped.

Stopped.

Seconds passed, seconds that became all of his life, and he began to know what he was seeing, began to understand what he saw and that was worse, so much worse that he wanted to make his mind freeze again.

He was sitting in a bushplane roaring seven thousand feet above the northern wilderness with a pilot who had suffered a massive heart attack and who was either dead or in something close to a coma.

He was alone.

In the roaring plane with no pilot he was alone.

Alone.

◀ *What problem does Brian face?*

Chapter 2

For a time that he could not understand Brian could do nothing. Even after his mind began working and he could see what had happened he could do nothing. It was as if his hands and arms were lead.

▶ What does Brian wish?

Then he looked for ways for it not to have happened. Be asleep, his mind screamed at the pilot. Just be asleep and your eyes will open now and your hands will take the controls and your feet will move to the pedals—but it did not happen.

The pilot did not move except that his head rolled on a neck impossibly loose as the plane hit a small bit of <u>turbulence</u>.

The plane.

Somehow the plane was still flying. Seconds had passed, nearly a minute, and the plane flew on as if nothing had happened and he had to do something, had to do something but did not know what.

Help.

He had to help.

He stretched one hand toward the pilot, saw that his fingers were trembling, and touched the pilot on the chest. He did not know what to do. He knew there were procedures, that you could do mouth-to-mouth

words for everyday use **tur • bu • lence** (tŭr′ byə lən[t]s) *n.,* violent, irregular motion or swirling agitation of water, air, or gas. *The pilot ordered the passengers to fasten their seatbelts because of the* <u>turbulence</u> *over the Rocky Mountains.*

on victims of heart attacks and push their chests—
C.P.R.[1]—but he did not know how to do it and in any
case could not do it with the pilot, who was sitting up
in the seat and still strapped in with his seatbelt. So he
touched the pilot with the tips of his fingers, touched
him on the chest and could feel nothing, no heartbeat, no rise and fall of breathing. Which meant that
the pilot was almost certainly dead.

"Please," Brian said. But did not know what or
who to ask. "Please . . ."

The plane lurched again, hit more turbulence, and
Brian felt the nose drop. It did not dive, but the nose
went down slightly and the down-angle increased
the speed, and he knew that at this angle, this slight
angle down, he would ultimately fly into the trees.
He could see them ahead on the horizon where
before he could see only sky.

He had to fly it somehow. Had to fly the plane. He
had to help himself. The pilot was gone, beyond anything he could do. He had to try and fly the plane.

◀ What does Brian have to do?

He turned back in the seat, facing the front, and put
his hands—still <u>trembling</u>—on the control wheel, his
feet gently on the rudder pedals. You pulled back on
the stick to raise the plane, he knew that from reading.
You always pulled back on the wheel. He gave it a tug
and it slid back toward him easily. Too easily. The
plane, with the increased speed from the tilt down,
swooped eagerly up and drove Brian's stomach down.
He pushed the wheel back in, went too far this time,
and the plane's nose went below the horizon and the
engine speed increased with the shallow dive.

Too much.

He pulled back again, more gently this time, and
the nose floated up again, too far but not as violently
as before, then down a bit too much, and up again,

◀ What does Brian do when he has steadied the plane?

---

1. **C.P.R.** Cardiopulmonary resuscitation: a procedure that may restore normal breathing after the heart stops

**words
for
everyday
use**   trem • ble (trem' bəl) v., shake involuntarily. *The dog cowered and <u>trembled</u> with fear.*

very easily, and the front of the engine cowling[2] set-tled. When he had it aimed at the horizon and it seemed to be steady, he held the wheel where it was, let out his breath—which he had been holding all this time—and tried to think what to do next.

It was a clear, blue-sky day with fluffy bits of clouds here and there and he looked out the window for a moment, hoping to see something, a town or village, but there was nothing. Just the green of the trees, endless green, and lakes scattered more and more thickly as the plane flew—where?

He was flying but did not know where, had no idea where he was going. He looked at the dashboard of the plane, studied the dials and hoped to get some help, hoped to find a compass, but it was all so con-fusing, a jumble of numbers and lights. One lighted display in the top center of the dashboard said the number 342, another next to it said 22. Down beneath that were dials with lines that seemed to indicate what the wings were doing, tipping or mov-ing, and one dial with a needle pointing to the num-ber 70, which he thought—only thought—might be the altimeter. The device that told him his height above the ground. Or above sea level. Somewhere he had read something about altimeters but he couldn't remember what, or where, or anything about them.

Slightly to the left and below the altimeter he saw a small rectangular panel with a lighted dial and two knobs. His eyes had passed over it two or three times before he saw what was written in tiny letters on top of the panel. Transmitter 221, was stamped in the metal and it hit him, finally, that this was the radio.

The radio. Of course. He had to use the radio. When the pilot had—had been hit that way (he couldn't bring himself to say that the pilot was dead, couldn't think it), he had been trying to use the radio.

Brian looked to the pilot. The headset was still on his head, turned sideways a bit from his jamming back into the seat, and the microphone switch was clipped into his belt.

---

2. **cowling.** Removable metal housing that covers an engine

Brian had to get the headset from the pilot. Had to reach over and get the headset from the pilot or he would not be able to use the radio to call for help. He had to reach over . . .

◀ Why doesn't Brian want to reach for the radio?

His hands began trembling again. He did not want to touch the pilot, did not want to reach for him. But he had to. Had to get the radio. He lifted his hands from the wheel, just slightly, and held them waiting to see what would happen. The plane flew on normally, smoothly.

All right, he thought. Now. Now to do this thing. He turned and reached for the headset, slid it from the pilot's head, one eye on the plane, waiting for it to dive. The headset came easily, but the microphone switch at the pilot's belt was jammed in and he had to pull to get it loose. When he pulled, his elbow bumped the wheel and pushed it in and the plane started down in a shallow dive. Brian grabbed the wheel and pulled it back, too hard again, and the plane went through another series of stomach-wrenching swoops up and down before he could get it under control.

When things had settled again he pulled at the mike cord once more and at last jerked the cord free. It took him another second or two to place the headset on his own head and position the small microphone tube in front of his mouth. He had seen the pilot use it, had seen him <u>depress</u> the switch at his belt, so Brian pushed the switch in and blew into the mike.

He heard the sound of his breath in the headset. "Hello! Is there anybody listening on this? Hello . . ."

He repeated it two or three times and then waited but heard nothing except his own breathing.

Panic came then. He had been afraid, had been stopped with the terror of what was happening, but now panic came and he began to scream into the microphone, scream over and over.

---

words for everyday use　　de • press (di pres') v., press down. <u>Depress</u> the knob to start the washer; pull out the knob to stop it.

"Help! Somebody help me! I'm in this plane and don't know . . . don't know . . . don't know . . ."

And he started crying with the screams, crying and slamming his hands against the wheel of the plane, causing it to jerk down, then back up. But again, he heard nothing but the sound of his own sobs in the microphone, his own screams <u>mocking</u> him, coming back into his ears.

The microphone. Awareness cut into him. He had used a CB radio in his uncle's pickup once. You had to turn the mike switch off to hear anybody else. He reached to his belt and released the switch.

For a second all he heard was the *whusssh* of the empty air waves. Then, through the noise and static he heard a voice.

"Whoever is calling on this radio net, I repeat, release your mike switch—you are covering me. You are covering me. Over."

It stopped and Brian hit his mike switch. "I hear you! I hear you. This is me . . . !" He released the switch.

"Roger. I have you now." The voice was very faint and breaking up. "Please state your difficulty and location. And say *over* to signal end of <u>transmission</u>. Over."

Please state my difficulty, Brian thought. God. My difficulty. "I am in a plane with a pilot who is—who has had a heart attack or something. He is—he can't fly. And I don't know how to fly. Help me. Help . . ." He turned his mike off without ending transmission properly.

There was a moment's hesitation before the answer. "Your signal is breaking up and I lost most of it. Understand . . . pilot . . . you can't fly. Correct? Over."

Brian could barely hear him now, heard mostly noise and static. "That's right. I can't fly. The plane is

▶ What previous experience helps Brian use the radio? What does he have to do?

words for everyday use

mock (mäk) v., mimic, imitate to make fun of. *Jordan laughed as he <u>mocked</u> Misha's actions.*

trans • mis • sion (tran[t]s mish' ən) n., act of sending a message. *The fax <u>transmission</u> failed because the line got disconnected.*

flying now but I don't know how much longer. Over."

". . . lost signal. Your location please. Flight number . . . location . . . ver."

"I don't know my flight number or location. I don't know anything. I told you that, over."

He waited now, waited but there was nothing. Once, for a second, he thought he heard a break in the noise, some part of a word, but it could have been static. Two, three minutes, ten minutes, the plane roared and Brian listened but heard no one. Then he hit the switch again.

"I do not know the flight number. My name is Brian Robeson and we left Hampton, New York headed for the Canadian oil fields to visit my father and I do not know how to fly an airplane and the pilot . . ."

He let go of the mike. His voice was starting to rattle and he felt as if he might start screaming at any second. He took a deep breath. "If there is anybody listening who can help me fly a plane, please answer."

Again he released the mike but heard nothing but the hissing of noise in the headset. After half an hour of listening and repeating the cry for help he tore the headset off in frustration and threw it to the floor. It all seemed so hopeless. Even if he did get somebody, what could anybody do? Tell him to be careful?

All so hopeless.

He tried to figure out the dials again. He thought he might know which was speed—it was a lighted number that read 160—but he didn't know if that was actual miles an hour, or kilometers, or if it just meant how fast the plane was moving through the air and not over the ground. He knew airspeed was different from groundspeed but not by how much.

Parts of books he'd read about flying came to him. How wings worked, how the propellor pulled the plane through the sky. Simple things that wouldn't help him now.

Nothing could help him now.

An hour passed. He picked up the headset and tried again—it was, he knew, in the end all he had—

◀ *What information does the person need? What information is Brian able to give?*

◀ *What kinds of information has Brian learned about planes from books? Why isn't this information helpful?*

but there was no answer. He felt like a prisoner, kept in a small cell that was <u>hurtling</u> through the sky at what he thought to be 160 miles an hour, headed—he didn't know where—just headed somewhere until . . .

There it was. Until what? Until he ran out of fuel. When the plane ran out of fuel it would go down.

Period.

Or he could pull the throttle[3] out and make it go down now. He had seen the pilot push the throttle in to increase speed. If he pulled the throttle back out, the engine would slow down and the plane would go down.

▶ What choices does Brian have?

Those were his choices. He could wait for the plane to run out of gas and fall or he could push the throttle in and make it happen sooner. If he waited for the plane to run out of fuel he would go farther—but he did not know which way he was moving. When the pilot had jerked he had moved the plane, but Brian could not remember how much or if it had come back to its original course. Since he did not know the original course anyway and could only guess at which display might be the compass—the one reading 342—he did not know where he had been or where he was going, so it didn't make much difference if he went down now or waited.

▶ What does Brian decide to do?

Everything in him <u>rebelled</u> against stopping the engine and falling now. He had a vague feeling that he was wrong to keep heading as the plane was heading, a feeling that he might be going off in the wrong direction, but he could not bring himself to stop the engine and fall. Now he was safe, or safer than if he went down—the plane was flying, he was still breathing. When the engine stopped he would go down.

---

3. **throttle.** Valve that controls how much fuel gets to an engine; also, the lever that controls this valve; equivalent to a gas pedal on a car—pushing in the throttle makes the plane go faster.

| **words for everyday use** | hur • tle (hʉrt′ əl) v., move quickly with a rushing sound. *The bottle hurtled through the air before crashing on the rock.* | re • bel (ri bel′) v., oppose or resist. *I tried to swallow the bug, but my stomach rebelled.* |

So he left the plane running, holding altitude, and kept trying the radio. He worked out a system. Every ten minutes by the small clock built into the dashboard he tried the radio with a simple message: "I need help. Is there anybody listening to me?"

In the times between transmissions he tried to prepare himself for what he knew was coming. When he ran out of fuel the plane would start down. He guessed that without the propellor pulling he would have to push the nose down to keep the plane flying—he thought he may have read that somewhere, or it just came to him. Either way it made sense. He would have to push the nose down to keep flying speed and then, just before he hit, he would have to pull the nose back up to slow the plane as much as possible.

It all made sense. Glide down, then slow the plane and hit.

Hit.

He would have to find a clearing as he went down. The problem with that was he hadn't seen one clearing since they'd started flying over the forest. Some swamps, but they had trees scattered through them. No roads, no trails, no clearings.

Just the lakes, and it came to him that he would have to use a lake for landing. If he went down in the trees he was certain to die. The trees would tear the plane to pieces as it went into them.

He would have to come down in a lake. No. On the edge of a lake. He would have to come down near the edge of a lake and try to slow the plane as much as possible just before he hit the water.

Easy to say, he thought, hard to do.

Easy say, hard do. Easy say, hard do. It became a chant that beat with the engine. Easy say, hard do.

Impossible to do.

He repeated the radio call seventeen times at the ten-minute <u>intervals</u>, working on what he would do

◀ *What plan does Brian make?*

between transmissions. Once more he reached over to the pilot and touched him on the face, but the skin was cold, hard cold, death cold, and Brian turned back to the dashboard. He did what he could, tightened his seatbelt, positioned himself, rehearsed mentally again and again what his <u>procedure</u> should be.

When the plane ran out of gas he should hold the nose down and head for the nearest lake and try to fly the plane kind of onto the water. That's how he thought of it. Kind of fly the plane onto the water. And just before it hit he should pull back on the wheel and slow the plane down to reduce the impact.

Over and over his mind ran the picture of how it would go. The plane running out of gas, flying the plane onto the water, the crash—from pictures he'd seen on television. He tried to visualize it. He tried to be ready.

But between the seventeenth and eighteenth radio transmissions, without a warning, the engine coughed, roared violently for a second and died. There was sudden silence, cut only by the sound of the windmilling propellor and the wind past the cockpit.

Brian pushed the nose of the plane down and threw up.

▶ *How does Brian react when the plane runs out of gas?*

words for everyday use

pro • ce • dure (prə sē′ jər) *n.*, series of steps for accomplishing something; usual way of doing something. *To ensure accurate results, each student must use the same procedure on the science class experiment.*

Chapter 3

Going to die, Brian thought. Going to die, gonna die, gonna die—his whole brain screamed it in the sudden silence.

Gonna die.

He wiped his mouth with the back of his arm and held the nose down. The plane went into a glide, a very fast glide that ate altitude, and suddenly there weren't any lakes. All he'd seen since they started flying over the forest was lakes and now they were gone. Gone. Out in front, far away at the horizon, he could see lots of them, off to the right and left more of them, glittering blue in the late afternoon sun.

◀ What is the first problem Brian has as he tries to follow his plan?

But he needed one right in front. He desperately needed a lake right in front of the plane and all he saw through the windshield were trees, green death trees. If he had to turn—if he had to turn he didn't think he could keep the plane flying. His stomach tightened into a series of rolling knots and his breath came in short bursts . . .

There!

Not quite in front but slightly to the right he saw a lake. L-shaped, with rounded corners, and the plane was nearly aimed at the long part of the L, coming from the bottom and heading to the top. Just a tiny bit to the right. He pushed the right rudder pedal gently and the nose moved over.

But the turn cost him speed and now the lake was above the nose. He pulled back on the wheel slightly

◀ What happens when Brian tries to turn the plane?

and the nose came up. This caused the plane to slow dramatically and almost seem to stop and <u>wallow</u> in the air. The controls became very loose-feeling and frightened Brian, making him push the wheel back in. This increased the speed a bit but filled the windshield once more with nothing but trees, and put the lake well above the nose and out of reach.

For a space of three or four seconds things seemed to hang, almost to stop. The plane was flying, but so slowly, so slowly . . . it would never reach the lake. Brian looked out to the side and saw a small pond and at the edge of the pond some large animal—he thought a moose—standing out in the water. All so still looking, so stopped, the pond and the moose and the trees, as he slid over them now only three or four hundred feet off the ground—all like a picture.

Then everything happened at once. Trees suddenly took on detail, filled his whole field of vision with green, and he knew he would hit and die, would die, but his luck held and just as he was to hit he came into an open lane, a channel of fallen trees, a wide place leading to the lake.

The plane, committed now to landing, to crashing, fell into the wide place like a stone, and Brian eased back on the wheel and braced himself for the crash. But there was a tiny bit of speed left and when he pulled on the wheel the nose came up and he saw in front the blue of the lake and at that instant the plane hit the trees.

There was a great <u>wrenching</u> as the wings caught the pines at the side of the clearing and broke back, ripping back just outside the main braces. Dust and dirt blew off the floor into his face so hard he thought there must have been some kind of explosion. He was momentarily blinded and slammed forward in his seat, smashing his head on the wheel.

Then a wild crashing sound, ripping of metal, and the plane rolled to the right and blew through the

▶ *Where does the plane crash? How does Brian react?*

words for everyday use	**wal • low** (wäl′ ō) *v.*, roll lazily or act helpless. *The small boat <u>wallowed</u> as it took on water.*	**wrench** (rench) *n.*, a sudden, sharp twist or pull. *Austin <u>wrenched</u> the car to the right to avoid hitting an unexpected hole in the road.*

trees, out over the water and down, down to slam into the lake, skip once on water as hard as concrete, water that tore the windshield out and shattered the side windows, water that drove him back into the seat. Somebody was screaming, screaming as the plane drove down into the water. Someone screamed tight animal screams of fear and pain and he did not know that it was his sound, that he roared against the water that took him and the plane still deeper, down in the water. He saw nothing but sensed blue, cold blue-green, and he raked at the seatbelt catch, tore his nails loose on one hand. He ripped at it until it released and somehow—the water trying to kill him, to end him—somehow he pulled himself out of the shattered front window and clawed up into the blue, felt something hold him back, felt his windbreaker tear and he was free. Tearing free. Ripping free.

◀ What does Brian have to do to survive?

But so far! So far to the surface and his lungs could not do this thing, could not hold and were through, and he sucked water, took a great pull of water that would—finally—win, finally take him, and his head broke into light and he vomited and swam, pulling without knowing what he was, what he was doing. Without knowing anything. Pulling until his hands caught at weeds and muck, pulling and screaming until his hands caught at last in grass and brush and he felt his chest on land, felt his face in the coarse blades of grass and he stopped, everything stopped. A color came that he had never seen before, a color that exploded in his mind with the pain and he was gone, gone from it all, spiraling out into the world, spiraling out into nothing.

Nothing.

Chapter 4

The memory was like a knife cutting into him. Slicing deep into him with hate.

The Secret.

He had been riding his ten-speed with a friend named Terry. They had been taking a run on a bike trail and decided to come back a different way, a way that took them past the Amber Mall. Brian remembered everything in incredible detail. Remembered the time on the bank clock in the mall, flashing 3:31, then the temperature, 82, and the date. All the numbers were part of the memory, all of his life was part of the memory.

Terry had just turned to smile at him about something and Brian looked over Terry's head and saw her.

His mother.

▶ Where did Brian see his mother? Who was with her?

She was sitting in a station wagon, a strange wagon. He saw her and she did not see him. Brian was going to wave or call out, but something stopped him. There was a man in the car.

Short blond hair, the man had. Wearing some kind of white pullover tennis shirt.

Brian saw this and more, saw the Secret and saw more later, but the memory came in pieces, came in scenes like this—Terry smiling, Brian looking over his head to see the station wagon and his mother sitting with the man, the time and temperature clock, the front wheel of his bike, the short blond hair of the man, the white shirt of the man, the hot-hate slices of the memory were exact.

The Secret.

Brian opened his eyes and screamed.

For seconds he did not know where he was, only that the crash was still happening and he was going to die, and he screamed until his breath was gone.

Then silence, filled with sobs as he pulled in air, half crying. How could it be so quiet? Moments ago there was nothing but noise, crashing and tearing, screaming, now quiet.

Some birds were singing.

How could birds be singing?

◀ Why do the singing birds seem strange to Brian?

His legs felt wet and he raised up on his hands and looked back down at them. They were in the lake. Strange. They went down into the water. He tried to move, but pain hammered into him and made his breath shorten into gasps and he stopped, his legs still in the water.

Pain.

Memory.

He turned again and sun came across the water, late sun, cut into his eyes and made him turn away.

It was over then. The crash.

He was alive.

The crash is over and I am alive, he thought. Then his eyes closed and he lowered his head for minutes that seemed longer. When he opened them again it was evening and some of the sharp pain had abated—there were many dull aches—and the crash came back to him fully.

Into the trees and out onto the lake. The plane had crashed and sunk in the lake and he had somehow pulled free.

He raised himself and crawled out of the water, grunting with the pain of movement. His legs were on fire, and his forehead felt as if somebody had been pounding on it with a hammer, but he could move. He pulled his legs out of the lake and crawled on his hands and knees until he was away from the wet-soft shore and near a small stand of brush of some kind.

◀ How does Brian feel when he tries to move?

Then he went down, only this time to rest, to save something of himself. He lay on his side and put his head on his arm and closed his eyes because that was all he could do now, all he could think of being able to do. He closed his eyes and slept, dreamless, deep and down.

▶ Why does Brian panic when he wakes up?

There was almost no light when he opened his eyes again. The darkness of night was thick and for a moment he began to panic again. To see, he thought. To see is everything. And he could not see. But he turned his head without moving his body and saw that across the lake the sky was a light gray, that the sun was starting to come up, and he remembered that it had been evening when he went to sleep.

"Must be morning now . . ." He mumbled it, almost in a hoarse whisper. As the thickness of sleep left him the world came back.

He was still in pain, all-over pain. His legs were cramped and drawn up, tight and aching, and his back hurt when he tried to move. Worst was a <u>keening</u> throb in his head that pulsed with every beat of his heart. It seemed that the whole crash had happened to his head.

▶ How does Brian assess his own injuries?

He rolled on his back and felt his sides and his legs, moving things slowly. He rubbed his arms; nothing seemed to be shattered or even sprained all that badly. When he was nine he had plowed his small dirt bike into a parked car and broken his ankle, had to wear a cast for eight weeks, and there was nothing now like that. Nothing broken. Just <u>battered</u> around a bit.

His forehead felt <u>massively</u> swollen to the touch, almost like a mound out over his eyes, and it was so tender that when his fingers grazed it he nearly cried. But there was nothing he could do about it and, like

---

words for everyday use

keen • ing (kēn′ iŋ) *adj.*, sharp; wailing. *The <u>keening</u> sound of wailing mourners filled the air.*

bat • ter (bat′ ər) *v.*, hit repeatedly, beat. *The hurricane winds <u>battered</u> the houses on the shore.*

mas • sive • ly (mas′ iv lē) *adv.*, hugely; severely. *My eyes were swollen so <u>massively</u> I couldn't see for three days.*

the rest of him, it seemed to be bruised more than broken.

I'm alive, he thought. I'm alive. It could have been different. There could have been death. I could have been done.

Like the pilot, he thought suddenly. The pilot in the plane, down into the water, down into the blue water strapped in the seat . . .

He sat up—or tried to. The first time he fell back. But on the second attempt, grunting with the effort, he managed to come to a sitting position and scrunched sideways until his back was against a small tree where he sat facing the lake, watching the sky get lighter and lighter with the coming dawn.

His clothes were wet and clammy and there was a faint chill. He pulled the torn remnants of his wind-breaker, pieces really, around his shoulders and tried to hold what heat his body could find. He could not think, could not make thought patterns work right. Things seemed to go back and forth between reality and imagination—except that it was all reality. One second he seemed only to have imagined that there was a plane crash, that he had fought out of the sinking plane and swum to shore; that it had all happened to some other person or in a movie playing in his mind. Then he would feel his clothes, wet and cold, and his forehead would slash a pain through his thoughts and he would know it was real, that it had really happened. But all in a haze, all in a haze-world. So he sat and stared at the lake, felt the pain come and go in waves, and watched the sun come over the end of the lake.

It took an hour, perhaps two—he could not measure time yet and didn't care—for the sun to get halfway up. With it came some warmth, small bits of it at first, and with the heat came clouds of insects—thick, swarming <u>hordes</u> of mosquitos that flocked to his body, made a living coat on his exposed skin,

◄ What does Brian have trouble with the morning after the crash?

words
for
everyday
use
    horde (hôrd) *n.,* swarm, crowd. *A <u>horde</u> of angry bees chased us after we upset their hive.*

clogged his nostrils when he inhaled, poured into his mouth when he opened it to take a breath.

It was not possibly believable. Not this. He had come through the crash, but the insects were not possible. He coughed them up, spat them out, sneezed them out, closed his eyes and kept brushing his face, slapping and crushing them by the dozens, by the hundreds. But as soon as he cleared a place, as soon as he killed them, more came, thick, whining, buzzing masses of them. Mosquitos and some small black flies he had never seen before. All biting, chewing, taking from him.

In moments his eyes were swollen shut and his face puffy and round to match his battered forehead. He pulled the torn pieces of his windbreaker over his head and tried to shelter in it but the jacket was full of rips and it didn't work. In desperation he pulled his T-shirt up to cover his face, but that exposed the skin of his lower back and the mosquitos and flies attacked the new soft flesh of his back so viciously that he pulled the shirt down.

In the end he sat with the windbreaker pulled up, brushed with his hands and took it, almost crying in frustration and <u>agony</u>. There was nothing left to do. And when the sun was fully up and heating him directly, bringing steam off of his wet clothes and bathing him with warmth, the mosquitos and flies disappeared. Almost that suddenly. One minute he was sitting in the middle of a swarm; the next, they were gone and the sun was on him.

Vampires, he thought. Apparently they didn't like the deep of night, perhaps because it was too cool, and they couldn't take the direct sunlight. But in that gray time in the morning, when it began to get warm and before the sun was full up and hot—he couldn't believe them. Never, in all the reading, in the movies he had watched on television about the outdoors, never once had they mentioned the mosquitos or

words for everyday use

ag • o • ny (ag' ə nē) *n.*, intense pain; distress. *Gil had known pain before, but never such <u>agony</u>.*

flies. All they ever showed on the <u>naturalist</u> shows was beautiful scenery or animals jumping around having a good time. Nobody ever mentioned mosquitoes and flies.

"Unnnhhh." He pulled himself up to stand against the tree and stretched, bringing new aches and pains. His back muscles must have been hurt as well—they almost seemed to tear when he stretched—and while the pain in his forehead seemed to be <u>abating</u> somewhat, just trying to stand made him weak enough to nearly collapse.

The backs of his hands were puffy and his eyes were almost swollen shut from the mosquitos, and he saw everything through a narrow squint.

Not that there was much to see, he thought, scratching the bites. In front of him lay the lake, blue and deep. He had a sudden picture of the plane, sunk in the lake, down and down in the blue with the pilot's body still strapped in the seat, his hair waving . . .

He shook his head. More pain. That wasn't something to think about.

He looked at his surroundings again. The lake stretched out slightly below him. He was at the base of the L, looking up the long part with the short part out to his right. In the morning light and calm the water was absolutely, perfectly still. He could see the reflections of the trees at the other end of the lake. Upside down in the water they seemed almost like another forest, an upside-down forest to match the real one. As he watched, a large bird—he thought it looked like a crow but it seemed larger—flew from the top, real forest, and the reflection-bird matched it, both flying out over the water.

Everything was green, so green it went into him. The forest was largely made up of pines and spruce, with stands of some low brush smeared here and

◄ *Describe in your own words or sketch the place where Brian is.*

---

words for everyday use

nat • u • ral • ist (nach′ rə ləst *or* nach′ ər ə ləst) *adj.*, related to the study of natural history or field biology. *The wildlife preserve has <u>naturalist</u> displays that give information about the animals.*

abate (ə bāt′) *v.*, decrease in intensity or amount. *When the storm <u>abates</u>, we'll go out and see how much damage has been done.*

there and thick grass and some other kind of very small brush all over. He couldn't identify most of it—except the evergreens—and some leafy trees he thought might be aspen. He'd seen pictures of aspens in the mountains on television. The country around the lake was moderately hilly, but the hills were small—almost <u>hummocks</u>—and there were very few rocks except to his left. There lay a rocky ridge that stuck out overlooking the lake, about twenty feet high.

If the plane had come down a little to the left it would have hit the rocks and never made the lake. He would have been smashed.

Destroyed.

The word came. I would have been destroyed and torn and smashed. Driven into the rocks and destroyed.

► What kind of luck does Brian think he has?

Luck, he thought. I have luck, I had good luck there. But he knew that was wrong. If he had had good luck his parents wouldn't have divorced because of the Secret and he wouldn't have been flying with a pilot who had a heart attack and he wouldn't be here where he had to have good luck to keep from being destroyed.

If you keep walking back from good luck, he thought, you'll come to bad luck.

He shook his head again—wincing. Another thing not to think about.

The rocky ridge was rounded and seemed to be of some kind of sandstone with bits of darker stone layered and stuck into it. Directly across the lake from it, at the inside corner of the L, was a mound of sticks and mud rising up out of the water a good eight or ten feet. At first Brian couldn't place it but knew that he somehow knew what it was—had seen it in films. Then a small brown head popped to the surface of the water near the mound and began swimming off down the short leg of the L leaving a V of ripples

---

words for everyday use

hum • mock (hum' ək) n., small, rounded hill. *The front yard is flat, but the back is filled with <u>hummocks</u>.*

behind and he remembered where he'd seen it. It was a beaver house, called a beaver lodge in a special he'd seen on the public channel.

A fish jumped. Not a large fish, but it made a big splash near the beaver, and as if by a signal there were suddenly little splops all over the sides of the lake—along the shore—as fish began jumping. Hundreds of them, jumping and slapping the water. Brian watched them for a time, still in the half-daze, still not thinking well. The scenery was very pretty, he thought, and there were new things to look at, but it was all a green and blue blur and he was used to the gray and black of the city, the sounds of the city. Traffic, people talking, sounds all the time—the hum and whine of the city.

◀ *How do the scenery and sounds differ from what Brian is used to?*

Here, at first, it was silent, or he thought it was silent, but when he started to listen, really listen, he heard thousands of things. Hisses and blurks, small sounds, birds singing, hum of insects, splashes from the fish jumping—there was great noise here, but a noise he did not know, and the colors were new to him, and the colors and noise mixed in his mind to make a green-blue blur that he could hear, hear as a hissing pulse-sound and he was still tired.

So tired.

So awfully tired, and standing had taken a lot of energy somehow, had drained him. He supposed he was still in some kind of shock from the crash and there was still the pain, the dizziness, the strange feeling.

He found another tree, a tall pine with no branches until the top, and sat with his back against it looking down on the lake with the sun warming him, and in a few moments he scrunched down and was asleep again.

Respond to the Selection

Think about the moment when Brian realizes the pilot is dead and he is alone in the plane. What would you think or do in his situation?

Investigate, Inquire, and Imagine

Recall: GATHER FACTS

1a. Why is Brian on the plane? What happens to the pilot?

2a. What did Brian see when he was riding his bike with Terry?

3a. What does Brian find unbelievable after surviving the plane crash?

Interpret: FIND MEANING

1b. What is Brian's main concern at the beginning of the flight? How does his focus change by the end of the flight?

2b. What do you think the Secret is? How does Brian feel about his mother?

3b. What other kinds of problems might Brian have in this environment?

Analyze: TAKE THINGS APART

4a. Brian says that if you keep walking back from good luck you come to bad luck. List examples of his good luck and of his bad luck in a chart like the one below.

Synthesize: BRING THINGS TOGETHER

4b. Overall, do you think Brian is more lucky or unlucky? Why?

Good Luck	Bad Luck

Perspective: LOOK AT OTHER VIEWS

5a. If you were Brian's mother or father, how would you feel when his plane did not arrive as scheduled?

Empathy: SEE FROM INSIDE

5b. Think about a time you were worried about somebody. Why were you worried? What did you do? What might you say to comfort Brian's mother or father?

Understanding Literature

PLOT AND INCITING INCIDENT. A **plot** is a series of events related to a central conflict, or struggle. The **inciting incident** is the event that introduces the central conflict. What is the inciting incident in *Hatchet*? What conflict does it introduce?

FLASHBACK. A **flashback** is a part of a story, poem, or play that presents events that happened at an earlier time. Chapter 4 starts with a flashback. What do you learn about Brian and his parents in the flashback? Why is this information important?

Chapter 5

His eyes snapped open, hammered open, and there were these things about himself that he knew, instantly.

▶ What does Brian know instantly upon waking up?

He was unbelievably, viciously thirsty. His mouth was dry and tasted foul and sticky. His lips were cracked and felt as if they were bleeding and if he did not drink some water soon he felt that he would <u>wither</u> up and die. Lots of water. All the water he could find.

He knew the thirst and felt the burn on his face. It was midafternoon and the sun had come over him and cooked him while he slept and his face was on fire, would blister, would peel. Which did not help the thirst, made it much worse. He stood, using the tree to pull himself up because there was still some pain and much stiffness, and looked down at the lake.

▶ What two things make Brian hesitate to drink the water?

It was water. But he did not know if he could drink it. Nobody had ever told him if you could or could not drink lakes. There was also the thought of the pilot.

Down in the blue with the plane, strapped in, the body . . .

Awful, he thought. But the lake was blue, and wet-looking, and his mouth and throat raged with the

---

words for everyday use
with • er (with′ ər) v., shrivel and lose strength. *Lack of water caused the plants to <u>wither</u>.*

thirst and he did not know where there might be another form of water he could drink. Besides, he had probably swallowed a ton of it while he was swimming out of the plane and getting to shore. In the movies they always showed the hero finding a clear spring with pure sweet water to drink but in the movies they didn't have plane wrecks and swollen foreheads and aching bodies and thirst that tore at the hero until he couldn't think.

◀ How does Brian's experience differ from a movie?

Brian took small steps down the bank to the lake. Along the edge there were thick grasses and the water looked a little <u>murky</u> and there were small things swimming in the water, small bugs. But there was a log extending about twenty feet out into the water of the lake—a beaver drop from some time before—with old limbs sticking up, almost like handles. He balanced on the log, holding himself up with the limbs, and teetered out past the weeds and murky water.

When he was out where the water was clear and he could see no bugs swimming he kneeled on the log to drink. A sip, he thought, still worrying about the lake water—I'll just take a sip.

But when he brought a cupped hand to his mouth and felt the cold lake water trickle past his cracked lips and over his tongue he could not stop. He had never, not even on long bike trips in the hot summer, been this thirsty. It was as if the water were more than water, as if the water had become all of life, and he could not stop. He stooped and put his mouth to the lake and drank and drank, pulling it deep and swallowing great gulps of it. He drank until his stomach was swollen, until he nearly fell off the log with it, then he rose and stagger-tripped his way back to the bank.

Where he was immediately sick and threw up most of the water. But his thirst was gone and the water seemed to reduce the pain in his head as well—although the sunburn still cooked his face.

◀ How do things improve once Brian drinks some water?

words for everyday use   murky (mur′ kē) adj., dark and obscure. The water was so <u>murky</u> we couldn't tell how deep the pond was.

"So." He almost jumped with the word, spoken aloud. It seemed so out of place, the sound. He tried it again. "So. So. So here I am."

And there it is, he thought. For the first time since the crash his mind started to work, his brain triggered and he began thinking.

Here I am—and where is that?

Where am I?

He pulled himself once more up the bank to the tall tree without branches and sat again with his back against the rough bark. It was hot now, but the sun was high and to his rear and he sat in the shade of the tree in <u>relative</u> comfort. There were things to sort out.

Here I am and that is nowhere. With his mind opened and thoughts happening it all tried to come in with a rush, all of what had occurred and he could not take it. The whole thing turned into a confused jumble that made no sense. So he fought it down and tried to take one thing at a time.

He had been flying north to visit his father for a couple of months, in the summer, and the pilot had had a heart attack and had died, and the plane had crashed somewhere in the Canadian north woods but he did not know how far they had flown or in what direction or where he was . . .

Slow down, he thought. Slow down more.

▶ *How does Brian simplify his situation?*

My name is Brian Robeson and I am thirteen years old and I am alone in the north woods of Canada.

All right, he thought, that's simple enough.

I was flying to visit my father and the plane crashed and sank in a lake.

There, keep it that way. Short thoughts.

I do not know where I am.

Which doesn't mean much. More to the point, *they* do not know where I am—*they* meaning anybody who might be wanting to look for me. The searchers.

words for everyday use

rel • a • tive (rel' ət iv) *adj.*, comparative. *The <u>relative</u> quiet of our town bothers some city dwellers.*

They would look for him, look for the plane. His father and mother would be frantic. They would tear the world apart to find him. Brian had seen searches on the news, seen movies about lost planes. When a plane went down they mounted <u>extensive</u> searches and almost always they found the plane within a day or two. Pilots all filed flight plans—a detailed plan for where and when they were going to fly, with all the courses explained. They would come, they would look for him. The searchers would get government planes and cover both sides of the flight plan filed by the pilot and search until they found him.

Maybe even today. They might come today. This was the second day after the crash. No. Brian frowned. Was it the first day or the second day? They had gone down in the afternoon and he had spent the whole night out cold. So this was the first real day. But they could still come today. They would have started the search immediately when Brian's plane did not arrive.

Yeah, they would probably come today.

Probably come in here with amphibious planes, small bushplanes with floats that could land right here on the lake and pick him up and take him home.

Which home? The father home or the mother home. He stopped the thinking. It didn't matter. Either on to his dad or back to his mother. Either way he would probably be home by late night or early morning, home where he could sit down and eat a large, cheesy, juicy burger with tomatoes and double fries with ketchup and a thick chocolate shake.

And there came hunger.

Brian rubbed his stomach. The hunger had been there but something else—fear, pain—had held it down. Now, with the thought of the burger, the emptiness roared at him. He could not believe the hunger, had never felt it this way. The lake water had

◀ What does Brian expect to happen?

◀ What does Brian imagine he will do that night or the next morning?

words for everyday use   **ex • ten • sive** (ik sten[t]′ siv) *adj.,* having a wide span or scope. *Due to the <u>extensive</u> changes we made, the new plan looks nothing like the old.*

filled his stomach but left it hungry, and now it demanded food, screamed for food.

And there was, he thought, absolutely nothing to eat.

Nothing.

▶ Brian again thinks of the movies. Why doesn't his knowledge of movies help him with his problem?

What did they do in the movies when they got stranded like this? Oh, yes, the hero usually found some kind of plant that he knew was good to eat and that took care of it. Just ate the plant until he was full or used some kind of cute trap to catch an animal and cook it over a slick little fire and pretty soon he had a full eight-course meal.

The trouble, Brian thought, looking around, was that all he could see was grass and brush. There was nothing obvious to eat and aside from about a million birds and the beaver he hadn't seen animals to trap and cook, and even if he got one somehow he didn't have any matches so he couldn't have a fire . . .

Nothing.

It kept coming back to that. He had nothing.

Well, almost nothing. As a matter of fact, he thought, I don't know what I've got or haven't got. Maybe I should try and figure out just how I stand. It will give me something to do—keep me from thinking of food. Until they come to find me.

Brian had once had an English teacher, a guy named Perpich, who was always talking about being positive, thinking positive, staying on top of things. That's how Perpich had put it—stay positive and stay on top of things. Brian thought of him now—wondered how to stay positive and stay on top of this. All Perpich would say is that I have to get <u>motivated</u>. He was always telling kids to get motivated.

Brian changed position so he was sitting on his knees. He reached into his pockets and took out everything he had and laid it on the grass in front of him.

▶ What does Brian find he has when he first checks?

It was pitiful enough. A quarter, three dimes, a nickel, and two pennies. A fingernail clipper. A bill-

---

words for everyday use

mo • ti • vate (mōt′ ə vāt) v., provide with need or desire to act. *Some people are <u>motivated</u> by the desire for fame and glory.*

fold with a twenty dollar bill—"In case you get stranded at the airport in some small town and have to buy food," his mother had said—and some odd pieces of paper.

And on his belt, somehow still there, the hatchet his mother had given him. He had forgotten it and now reached around and took it out and put it in the grass. There was a touch of rust already forming on the cutting edge of the blade and he rubbed it off with his thumb.

That was it.

He frowned. No, wait—if he was going to play the game, might as well play it right. Perpich would tell him to quit messing around. Get motivated. Look at *all* of it, Robeson.

He had on a pair of good tennis shoes, now almost dry. And socks. And jeans and underwear and a thin leather belt and a T-shirt with a windbreaker so torn it hung on him in tatters.

◄ What else does he realize he has?

And a watch. He had a digital watch still on his wrist but it was broken from the crash—the little screen blank—and he took it off and almost threw it away but stopped the hand motion and lay the watch on the grass with the rest of it.

There. That was it.

No, wait. One other thing. Those were all the things he had, but he also had himself. Perpich used to drum that into them—"You are your most valuable <u>asset</u>. Don't forget that. *You* are the best thing you have."

Brian looked around again. I wish you were here, Perpich. I'm hungry and I'd trade everything I have for a hamburger.

"I'm hungry." He said it aloud. In normal tones at first, then louder and louder until he was yelling it. "I'm hungry, I'm hungry, I'm hungry!"

When he stopped there was sudden silence, not just from him but the clicks and blurps and bird

words for everyday use   as • set (as′ et) *n.*, resource. *A sense of humor is an <u>asset</u> when dealing with difficult situations.*

sounds of the forest as well. The noise of his voice had startled everything and it was quiet. He looked around, listened with his mouth open, and realized that in all his life he had never heard silence before. Complete silence. There had always been some sound, some kind of sound.

It lasted only a few seconds, but it was so intense that it seemed to become part of him. Nothing. There was no sound. Then the bird started again, and some kind of buzzing insect, and then a chattering and a cawing, and soon there was the same background of sound.

Which left him still hungry.

▶ What attitude does Brian take toward his hunger?

Of course, he thought, putting the coins and the rest back in his pocket and the hatchet in his belt—of course if they come tonight or even if they take as long as tomorrow the hunger is no big thing. People have gone for many days without food as long as they've got water. Even if they don't come until late tomorrow I'll be all right. Lose a little weight, maybe, but the first hamburger and a malt and fries will bring it right back.

A mental picture of a hamburger, the way they showed it in the television commercials, thundered into his thoughts. Rich colors, the meat juicy and hot . . .

He pushed the picture away. So even if they didn't find him until tomorrow, he thought, he would be all right. He had plenty of water, although he wasn't sure if it was good and clean or not.

He sat again by the tree, his back against it. There was a thing bothering him. He wasn't quite sure what it was but it kept chewing at the edge of his thoughts. Something about the plane and the pilot that would change things. . .

▶ What does Brian remember happening when the pilot had his heart attack? How might this action have affected Brian's chances of being rescued?

Ahh, there it was—the moment when the pilot had his heart attack his right foot had jerked down on the rudder pedal and the plane had slewed sideways. What did that mean? Why did that keep coming into his thinking that way, nudging and pushing?

It means, a voice in his thoughts said, that they might not be coming for you tonight or even tomorrow. When the pilot pushed the rudder pedal the plane had jerked to the side and <u>assumed</u> a new course. Brian could not remember how much it had pulled around, but it wouldn't have had to be much because after that, with the pilot dead, Brian had flown for hour after hour on the new course.

Well away from the flight plan the pilot had filed. Many hours, at maybe 160 miles an hour. Even if it was only a little off course, with that speed and time Brian might now be sitting several hundred miles off to the side of the recorded flight plan.

And they would probably search most heavily at first along the flight plan course. They might go out to the side a little, but he could easily be three, four hundred miles to the side. He could not know, could not think of how far he might have flown wrong because he didn't know the original course and didn't know how much they had pulled sideways.

Quite a bit—that's how he remembered it. Quite a jerk to the side. It pulled his head over sharply when the plane had swung around.

They might not find him for two or three days. He felt his heartbeat increase as the fear started. The thought was there but he fought it down for a time, pushed it away, then it exploded out.

◀ What does Brian have to admit about his chances of being rescued?

They might not find him for a long time.

And the next thought was there as well, that they might never find him, but that was panic and he fought it down and tried to stay positive. They searched hard when a plane went down, they used many men and planes and they would go to the side, they would know he was off from the flight path, he had talked to the man on the radio, they would somehow know . . .

It would be all right.

They would find him. Maybe not tomorrow, but soon. Soon. Soon.

They would find him soon.

---

words for everyday use

as • sume (ə süm') v., take on. *Tyrone <u>assumed</u> leadership of the group when Raisa resigned.*

▶ What does Brian need to do?

Gradually, like sloshing oil his thoughts settled back and the panic was gone. Say they didn't come for two days—no, say they didn't come for three days, even push that to four days—he could live with that. He would have to live with that. He didn't want to think of them taking longer. But say four days. He had to do something. He couldn't just sit at the bottom of this tree and stare down at the lake for four days.

And nights. He was in deep woods and didn't have any matches, couldn't make a fire. There were large things in the woods. There were wolves, he thought, and bears—other things. In the dark he would be in the open here, just sitting at the bottom of a tree.

He looked around suddenly, felt the hair on the back of his neck go up. Things might be looking at him right now, waiting for him—waiting for dark so they could move in and take him.

He fingered the hatchet at his belt. It was the only weapon he had, but it was something.

▶ What two things does Brian need?

He had to have some kind of shelter. No, make that more: He had to have some kind of shelter and he had to have something to eat.

He pulled himself to his feet and jerked the back of his shirt down before the mosquitos could get at it. He had to do something to help himself.

I have to get motivated, he thought, remembering Perpich. Right now I'm all I've got. I have to do something.

Chapter 6

Two years before he and Terry had been fooling around down near the park, where the city seemed to end for a time and the trees grew thick and came down to the small river that went through the park. It was thick there and seemed kind of wild, and they had been joking and making things up and they pretended that they were lost in the woods and talked in the afternoon about what they would do. Of course they figured they'd have all sorts of goodies like a gun and a knife and fishing gear and matches so they could hunt and fish and have a fire.

I wish you were here, Terry, he thought. With a gun and a knife and some matches . . .

In the park that time they had decided the best shelter was a lean-to[1] and Brian set out now to make one up. Maybe cover it with grass or leaves or sticks, he thought, and he started to go down to the lake again, where there were some willows he could cut down for braces. But it struck him that he ought to find a good place for the lean-to and so he decided to look around first. He wanted to stay near the lake because he thought the plane, even deep in the water, might show up to somebody flying over and

◄ How had Brian felt about the idea of being lost in the woods when he and Terry talked about it?

◄ Why does Brian want to stay near the lake?

---

1. **lean-to.** Rough shelter with a roof that slopes on one side

he didn't want to <u>diminish</u> any chance he might have of being found.

His eyes fell upon the stone ridge to his left and he thought at first he should build his shelter against the stone. But before that he decided to check out the far side of the ridge and that was where he got lucky.

Using the sun and the fact that it rose in the east and set in the west, he decided that the far side was the northern side of the ridge. At one time in the far past it had been scooped by something, probably a glacier,[2] and this scooping had left a kind of sideways bowl, back in under a ledge. It wasn't very deep, not a cave, but it was smooth and made a perfect roof and he could almost stand in under the ledge. He had to hold his head slightly tipped forward at the front to keep it from hitting the top. Some of the rock that had been scooped out had also been <u>pulverized</u> by the glacial action, turned into sand, and now made a small sand beach that went down to the edge of the water in front and to the right of the overhang.

It was his first good luck.

No, he thought. He had good luck in the landing. But this was good luck as well, luck he needed.

All he had to do was wall off part of the bowl and leave an opening as a doorway and he would have a perfect shelter—much stronger than a lean-to and dry because the overhang made a watertight roof.

He crawled back in, under the ledge, and sat. The sand was cool here in the shade, and the coolness felt wonderful to his face, which was already starting to blister and get especially painful on his forehead, with the blisters on top of the swelling.

He was also still weak. Just the walk around the back of the ridge and the slight climb over the top had left his legs rubbery. It felt good to sit for a bit under the shade of the overhang in the cool sand.

▶ *Where does Brian decide to build his shelter?*

---

2. **glacier.** Large body of ice that moves over land

words for everyday use

di • min • ish (də min′ ish) *v.,* lessen. *The opposing team's fifth soccer goal <u>diminished</u> our hopes of a comeback.*

pul • ver • ize (pul′ və rīz) *v.,* crush or grind into powder. *The cookies were <u>pulverized</u> by the weight of the books in my bag.*

And now, he thought, if I just had something to eat.

Anything.

When he had rested a bit he went back down to the lake and drank a couple of swallows of water. He wasn't all that thirsty but he thought the water might help to take the edge off his hunger. It didn't. Somehow the cold lake water actually made it worse, sharpened it.

He thought of dragging in wood to make a wall on part of the overhang, and picked up one piece to pull up, but his arms were too weak and he knew that it wasn't just the crash and injury to his body and head, it was also that he was weak from hunger.

He would have to find something to eat. Before he did anything else he would have to have something to eat.

But what?

Brian leaned against the rock and stared out at the lake. What, in all of this, was there to eat? He was so used to having food just be there, just always being there. When he was hungry he went to the icebox,[3] or to the store, or sat down at a meal his mother cooked.

◀ *What is Brian used to doing when he is hungry?*

Oh, he thought, remembering a meal now—oh. It was the last Thanksgiving, last year, the last Thanksgiving they had as a family before his mother demanded the divorce and his father moved out in the following January. Brian already knew the Secret but did not know it would cause them to break up and thought it might work out, the Secret that his father still did not know but that he would try to tell him. When he saw him.

The meal had been turkey and they cooked it in the back yard in the barbecue over charcoal with the lid down tight. His father had put hickory chips on the charcoal and the smell of the cooking turkey and the hickory smoke had filled the yard. When his father took the lid off, smiling, the smell that had come out was unbelievable, and when they sat to eat the meat was wet with juice and rich and had the taste of the smoke in it . . .

---

3. **icebox.** Refrigerator

He had to stop this. His mouth was full of saliva and his stomach was twisting and growling.

What was there to eat?

What had he read or seen that told him about food in the wilderness? Hadn't there been something? A show, yes, a show on television about air force pilots and some kind of course they took. A survival course. All right, he had the show coming into his thoughts now. The pilots had to live in the desert. They put them in the desert down in Arizona or someplace and they had to live for a week. They had to find food and water for a week.

For water they had made a sheet of plastic into a dew-gathering device and for food they ate lizards.

▶ How does something Brian watched on TV help him figure out how to find food?

That was it. Of course Brian had lots of water and there weren't too many lizards in the Canadian woods, that he knew. One of the pilots had used a watch crystal as a magnifying glass to focus the sun and start a fire so they didn't have to eat the lizards raw. But Brian had a digital watch, without a crystal, broken at that. So the show didn't help him much.

Wait, there was one thing. One of the pilots, a woman, had found some kind of beans on a bush and she had used them with her lizard meat to make a little stew in a tin can she had found. Bean lizard stew. There weren't any beans here, but there must be berries. There had to be berry bushes around. Sure, the woods were full of berry bushes. That's what everybody always said. Well, he'd actually never heard anybody *say* it. But he felt that it should be true.

There must be berry bushes.

He stood and moved out into the sand and looked up at the sun. It was still high. He didn't know what time it must be. At home it would be one or two if the sun were that high. At home at one or two his mother would be putting away the lunch dishes and getting ready for her exercise class. No, that would have been yesterday. Today she would be going to see *him*. Today was Thursday and she always went to see him on Thursdays. Wednesday was the exercise class and Thursdays she went to see him. Hot little jets of hate worked into his thoughts, pushed once, moved

▶ What kind of thinking does Brian need to stop?

back. If his mother hadn't begun to see *him* and forced the divorce, Brian wouldn't be here now.

He shook his head. Had to stop that kind of thinking. The sun was still high and that meant that he had some time before darkness to find berries. He didn't want to be away from his—he almost thought of it as home—shelter when it came to be dark.

He didn't want to be anywhere in the woods when it came to be dark. And he didn't want to get lost—which was a real problem. All he knew in the world was the lake in front of him and the hill at his back and the ridge—if he lost sight of them there was a really good chance that he would get turned around and not find his way back.

So he had to look for berry bushes, but keep the lake or the rock ridge in sight at all times.

He looked up the lake shore, to the north. For a good distance, perhaps two hundred yards, it was fairly clear. There were tall pines, the kind with no limbs until very close to the top, with a gentle breeze sighing in them, but not too much low brush. Two hundred yards up there seemed to be a belt of thick, lower brush starting—about ten or twelve feet high—and that formed a wall he could not see through. It seemed to go on around the lake, thick and lushly green, but he could not be sure.

If there were berries they would be in that brush, he felt, and as long as he stayed close to the lake, so he could keep the water on his right and know it was there, he wouldn't get lost. When he was done or found berries, he thought, he would just turn around so the water was on his left and walk back until he came to the ridge and his shelter.

◀ *What does Brian do so he doesn't get lost?*

Simple. Keep it simple. I am Brian Robeson. I have been in a plane crash. I am going to find some food. I am going to find berries.

He walked slowly—still a bit pained in his joints and weak from hunger—up along the side of the lake. The trees were full of birds singing ahead of him in the sun. Some he knew, some he didn't. He saw a robin, and some kind of sparrows, and a flock of reddish orange birds with thick beaks. Twenty or thirty of them were sitting in one of the pines. They made much noise and flew away ahead of him when he walked under the tree. He watched them fly, their color a bright slash in solid green, and in this way he found the berries. The birds landed in some taller willow type of undergrowth with wide leaves and started jumping and making noise. At first he was too far away to see what they were doing, but their color drew him and he moved toward them, keeping the lake in sight on his right, and when he got closer he saw they were eating berries.

▶ What helps point Brian to the berries?

He could not believe it was that easy. It was as if the birds had taken him right to the berries. The slender branches went up about twenty feet and were heavy, drooping with clusters of bright red berries. They were half as big as grapes but hung in bunches much like grapes and when Brian saw them, <u>glistening</u> red in the sunlight, he almost yelled.

His pace quickened and he was in them in moments, scattering the birds, grabbing branches, stripping them to fill his mouth with berries.

▶ What were the berries like?

He almost spit them out. It wasn't that they were bitter so much as that they lacked any sweetness, had a tart flavor that left his mouth dry feeling. And they were like cherries in that they had large pits, which made them hard to chew. But there was such a hunger on him, such an emptiness, that he could not stop and kept stripping branches and eating berries by the handful, grabbing and jamming them into his mouth and swallowing them pits and all.

He could not stop and when, at last, his stomach was full he was still hungry. Two days without food must have shrunken his stomach, but the drive of hunger was still there. Thinking of the birds, and how they would come back into the berries when he left, he made a carrying pouch of his torn windbreaker and kept picking. Finally, when he judged he had close to four pounds in the jacket he stopped and went back to his camp by the ridge.

---

words for everyday use

glis • ten (glis′ ən) v., sparkle; give off a reflection like a polished surface. *The dew on the grass glistened in the sunlight.*

Now, he thought. Now I have some food and I can do something about fixing this place up. He glanced at the sun and saw he had some time before dark.

If only I had matches, he thought, looking <u>ruefully</u> at the beach and lakeside. There was driftwood everywhere, not to mention dead and dry wood all over the hill and dead-dry branches hanging from every tree. All firewood. And no matches. How did they used to do it? he thought. Rub two sticks together?

He tucked the berries in the pouch back in under the overhang in the cool shade and found a couple of sticks. After ten minutes of rubbing he felt the sticks and they were almost cool to the touch. Not that, he thought. They didn't do fire that way. He threw the sticks down in disgust. So no fire. But he could still fix the shelter and make it—here the word "safer" came into his mind and he didn't know why—more livable.

Kind of close it in, he thought. I'll just close it in a bit.

He started dragging sticks up from the lake and pulling long dead branches down from the hill, never getting out of sight of the water and the ridge. With these he <u>interlaced</u> and wove a wall across the opening of the front of the rock. It took over two hours, and he had to stop several times because he still felt a bit weak and once because he felt a strange new twinge in his stomach. A tightening, rolling. Too many berries, he thought. I ate too many of them.

But it was gone soon and he kept working until the entire front of the overhang was covered save for a small opening at the right end, nearest the lake. The doorway was about three feet, and when he went in he found himself in a room almost fifteen feet long and eight to ten feet deep, with the rock wall sloping down at the rear.

"Good," he said, nodding. "Good . . ."

Outside the sun was going down, finally, and in the initial coolness the mosquitos came out again

◄ How does Brian try to make fire? What are the results?

◄ What happens when the sun goes down?

words for everyday use	rue • ful • ly (rü′ fə lē) *adv.*, mournfully, regretfully. *Lou ran through the rain, <u>ruefully</u> remembering that he had left his umbrella at home.*	in • ter • lace (int ər lās′) *v.*, connect by crossing or alternating. <u>*Interlace*</u> *your fingers to give me a boost up.*

and clouded in on him. They were thick, terrible, if not quite as bad as in the morning, and he kept brushing them off his arms until he couldn't stand it and then dumped the berries and put the torn windbreaker on. At least the sleeves covered his arms.

Wrapped in the jacket, with darkness coming down fast now, he crawled back in under the rock and huddled and tried to sleep. He was deeply tired, and still aching some, but sleep was slow coming and did not finally settle in until the evening cool turned to night cool and the mosquitos slowed.

Then, at last, with his stomach turning on the berries, Brian went to sleep.

Chapter 7

"Mother!"

He screamed it and he could not be sure if the scream awakened him or the pain in his stomach. His whole abdomen was torn with great rolling jolts of pain, pain that doubled him in the darkness of the little shelter, put him over and face down in the sand to moan again and again: "Mother, mother, mother . . ."

Never anything like this. Never. It was as if all the berries, all the pits had exploded in the center of him, ripped and tore at him. He crawled out the doorway and was sick in the sand, then crawled still farther and was sick again, vomiting and with terrible diarrhea for over an hour, for over a year he thought, until he was at last empty and drained of all strength.

◀ *What makes Brian sick?*

Then he crawled back into the shelter and fell again to the sand but could not sleep at first, could do nothing except lie there, and his mind decided then to bring the memory up again.

In the mall. Every detail. His mother sitting in the station wagon with the man. And she had leaned across and kissed him, kissed the man with the short blond hair, and it was not a friendly peck, but a kiss. A kiss where she turned her head over at an angle and put her mouth against the mouth of the blond man who was not his father and kissed, mouth to mouth, and then brought her hand up to touch his

◀ *What is the Secret?*

cheek, his forehead, while they were kissing. And Brian saw it.

Saw this thing that his mother did with the blond man. Saw the kiss that became the Secret that his father still did not know about, know all about.

The memory was so real that he could feel the heat in the mall that day, could remember the worry that Terry would turn and see his mother, could remember the worry of the shame of it and then the memory faded and he slept again . . .

Awake.

For a second, perhaps two, he did not know where he was, was still in his sleep somewhere. Then he saw the sun streaming in the open doorway of the shelter and heard the close, vicious whine of the mosquitos and knew. He brushed his face, completely welted now with two days of bites, completely covered with lumps and bites, and was surprised to find the swelling on his forehead had gone down a great deal, was almost gone.

The smell was awful and he couldn't place it. Then he saw the pile of berries at the back of the shelter and remembered the night and being sick.

"Too many of them," he said aloud. "Too many gut cherries . . ."

He crawled out of the shelter and found where he'd messed the sand. He used sticks and cleaned it as best he could, covered it with clean sand and went down to the lake to wash his hands and get a drink.

▶ How does Brian look?

It was still very early, only just past true dawn, and the water was so calm he could see his reflection. It frightened him—the face was cut and bleeding, swollen and lumpy, the hair all matted, and on his forehead a cut had healed but left the hair stuck with blood and scab. His eyes were slits in the bites and he was—somehow—covered with dirt. He slapped the water with his hand to destroy the mirror.

Ugly, he thought. Very, very ugly.

And he was, at that moment, almost overcome with self-pity. He was dirty and starving and bitten and hurt and lonely and ugly and afraid and so completely miserable that it was like being in a pit, a dark, deep pit with no way out.

He sat back on the bank and fought crying. Then let it come and cried for perhaps three, four minutes. Long tears, self-pity tears, wasted tears.

He stood, went back to the water, and took small drinks. As soon as the cold water hit his stomach he felt the hunger sharpen, as it had before, and he stood and held his abdomen until the hunger cramps <u>receded</u>.

He had to eat. He was weak with it again, down with the hunger, and he had to eat.

Back at the shelter the berries lay in a pile where he had dumped them when he grabbed his wind-breaker—gut cherries he called them in his mind now—and he thought of eating some of them. Not such a crazy amount, as he had, which he felt brought on the sickness in the night—but just enough to stave off the hunger a bit.

◀ Why does Brian eat more of the "gut cherries"? What steps does he take to try to avoid getting sick again?

He crawled into the shelter. Some flies were on the berries and he brushed them off. He selected only the berries that were solidly ripe—not the light red ones, but the berries that were dark, maroon red to black and swollen in ripeness. When he had a small hand-ful of them he went back down to the lake and washed them in the water—small fish scattered away when he splashed the water up and he wished he had a fishing line and hook—then he ate them carefully, spitting out the pits. They were still tart, but had a sweetness to them, although they seemed to make his lips a bit numb.

When he finished he was still hungry, but the edge was gone and his legs didn't feel as weak as they had.

He went back to the shelter. It took him half an hour to go through the rest of the berries and sort them, putting all the fully ripe ones in a pile on some leaves, the rest in another pile. When he was done he covered the two piles with grass he tore

words for everyday use   re • cede (ri sēd´) v., move back or decrease. *My fear <u>receded</u> as daylight came.*

from the lake shore to keep the flies off and went back outside.

They were awful berries, those gut cherries, he thought. But there was food there, food of some kind, and he could eat a bit more later tonight if he had to.

For now he had a full day ahead of him. He looked at the sky through the trees and saw that while there were clouds, they were scattered and did not seem to hold rain. There was a light breeze that seemed to keep the mosquitos down and, he thought, looking up along the lake shore, if there was one kind of berry there should be other kinds. Sweeter kinds.

▶ What does Brian call his shelter?

If he kept the lake in sight as he had done yesterday he should be all right, should be able to find home again—and it stopped him. He had actually thought it that time.

Home. Three days, no, two—or was it three? Yes, this was the third day and he had thought of the shelter as home.

He turned and looked at it, studied the <u>crude</u> work. The brush made a fair wall, not weathertight but it cut most of the wind off. He hadn't done so badly at that. Maybe it wasn't much, but also maybe it was all he had for a home.

All right, he thought, so I'll call it home.

He turned back and set off up the side of the lake, heading for the gut cherry bushes, his windbreaker-bag in his hand. Things were bad, he thought, but maybe not that bad.

Maybe he could find some better berries.

When he came to the gut cherry bushes he paused. The branches were empty of birds but still had many berries, and some of those that had been merely red yesterday were now a dark maroon to black. Much riper. Maybe he should stay and pick them to save them.

---

words for everyday use **crude** (krüd) *n.*, rough. *Although the <u>crude</u> drawing of the room lacked detail, it gave us some idea about where we could place the furniture.*

But the explosion in the night was still much in his memory and he decided to go on. Gut cherries were food, but tricky to eat. He needed something better.

Another hundred yards up the shore there was a place where the wind had torn another path. These must have been fierce winds, he thought, to tear places up like this—as they had the path he had found with the plane when he crashed. Here the trees were not all the way down but twisted and snapped off halfway up from the ground, so their tops were all down and rotted and gone, leaving the snags poking into the sky like broken teeth. It made for tons of dead and dry wood and he wished once more he could get a fire going. It also made a kind of clearing—with the tops of the trees gone the sun could get down to the ground—and it was filled with small thorny bushes that were covered with berries.

◀ What caused the clearing in the woods? What does Brian find in the clearing?

Raspberries.

These he knew because there were some raspberry bushes in the park and he and Terry were always picking and eating them when they biked past.

The berries were full and ripe, and he tasted one to find it sweet, and with none of the problems of the gut cherries. Although they did not grow in clusters, there were many of them and they were easy to pick and Brian smiled and started eating.

Sweet juice, he thought. Oh, they were sweet with just a tiny tang and he picked and ate and picked and ate and thought that he had never tasted anything this good. Soon, as before, his stomach was full, but now he had some sense and he did not gorge or cram more down. Instead he picked more and put them in his windbreaker, feeling the morning sun on his back and thinking he was rich, rich with food now, just rich, and he heard a noise to his rear, a slight noise, and he turned and saw the bear.

◀ What does Brian see while picking berries?

He could do nothing, think nothing. His tongue, stained with berry juice, stuck to the roof of his mouth and he stared at the bear. It was black, with a cinnamon-colored nose, not twenty feet from him and big. No, huge. It was all black fur and huge. He had seen one in the zoo in the city once, a black bear, but it had been from India or somewhere. This one was wild, and much bigger than the one in the zoo and it was right there.

Right there.

The sun caught the ends of the hairs along his back. Shining black and silky the bear stood on its hind legs, half up, and studied Brian, just studied him, then lowered itself and moved slowly to the left, eating berries as it rolled along, wuffling and delicately using its mouth to lift each berry from the stem, and in seconds it was gone. Gone, and Brian still had not moved. His tongue was stuck to the top of his mouth, the tip half out, his eyes were wide and his hands were reaching for a berry.

Then he made a sound, a low: "Nnnnnnggg." It made no sense, was just a sound of fear, of disbelief that something that large could have come so close to him without his knowing. It just walked up to him and could have eaten him and he could have done nothing. Nothing. And when the sound was half done a thing happened with his legs, a thing he had nothing to do with, and they were running in the opposite direction from the bear, back toward the shelter.

He would have run all the way, in panic, but after he had gone perhaps fifty yards his brain took over and slowed and, finally, stopped him.

If the bear had wanted you, his brain said, he would have taken you. It is something to understand, he thought, not something to run away from. The bear was eating berries.

Not people.

The bear made no move to hurt you, to threaten you. It stood to see you better, study you, then went on its way eating berries. It was a big bear, but it did not want you, did not want to cause you harm, and that is the thing to understand here.

He turned and looked back at the stand of raspberries. The bear was gone, the birds were singing, he saw nothing that could hurt him. There was no danger here that he could sense, could feel. In the city, at night, there was sometimes danger. You could not be in the park at night, after dark, because of the danger.

▶ Why does Brian stop running toward the shelter?

But here, the bear had looked at him and had moved on and—this filled his thoughts—the berries were so good.

So good. So sweet and rich and his body was so empty.

And the bear had almost <u>indicated</u> that it didn't mind sharing—had just walked from him.

And the berries were so good.

And, he thought, finally, if he did not go back and get the berries he would have to eat the gut cherries again tonight.

That convinced him and he walked slowly back to the raspberry patch and continued picking for the entire morning, although with great caution, and once when a squirrel rustled some pine needles at the base of a tree he nearly jumped out of his skin.

About noon—the sun was almost straight overhead—the clouds began to thicken and look dark. In moments it started to rain and he took what he had picked and trotted back to the shelter. He had eaten probably two pounds of raspberries and had maybe another three pounds in his jacket, rolled in a pouch.

He made it to the shelter just as the clouds completely opened and the rain roared down in sheets. Soon the sand outside was drenched and there were <u>rivulets</u> running down to the lake. But inside he was dry and snug. He started to put the picked berries back in the sorted pile with the gut cherries but noticed that the raspberries were seeping through the jacket. They were much softer than the gut cherries and apparently were being crushed a bit with their own weight.

When he held the jacket up and looked beneath it he saw a stream of red liquid. He put a finger in it and found it to be sweet and tangy, like pop without the fizz, and he grinned and lay back on the sand, holding the bag up over his face and letting the seepage drip into his mouth.

---

words for everyday use

in • di • cate (in' də kāt) *v.*, demonstrate or show by sign. *Trinh nodded to <u>indicate</u> she understood.*

riv • u • let (riv' yə lət) *n.*, small stream. *After the heavy rain, <u>rivulets</u> ran across the parched land.*

▶ *Assess Brian's state of mind at this point in the story.*

Outside the rain poured down, but Brian lay back, drinking the syrup from the berries, dry and with the pain almost all gone, the stiffness also gone, his belly full and a good taste in his mouth.

For the first time since the crash he was not thinking of himself, of his own life. Brian was wondering if the bear was as surprised as he to find another being in the berries.

Later in the afternoon, as evening came down, he went to the lake and washed the sticky berry juice from his face and hands, then went back to prepare for the night.

While he had accepted and understood that the bear did not want to hurt him, it was still much in his thoughts and as darkness came into the shelter he took the hatchet out of his belt and put it by his head, his hand on the handle, as the day caught up with him and he slept.

Chapter 8

At first he thought it was a growl. In the still darkness of the shelter in the middle of the night his eyes came open and he was awake and he thought there was a growl. But it was the wind, a medium wind in the pines had made some sound that brought him up, brought him awake. He sat up and was hit with the smell.

It terrified him. The smell was one of rot, some musty rot that made him think only of graves with cobwebs and dust and old death. His nostrils widened and he opened his eyes wider but he could see nothing. It was too dark, too hard dark with clouds covering even the small light from the stars, and he could not see. But the smell was alive, alive and full and in the shelter. He thought of the bear, thought of Bigfoot and every monster he had ever seen in every fright movie he had ever watched, and his heart hammered in his throat.

Then he heard the <u>slithering</u>. A brushing sound, a slithering brushing sound near his feet—and he kicked out as hard as he could, kicked out and threw the hatchet at the sound, a noise coming from his throat. But the hatchet missed, sailed into the wall

◀ What is Brian afraid of?

◀ What happens when Brian throws the hatchet?

words for everyday use   slith • er • ing (slith′ ər iŋ) *n.*, sliding movement or sound. *When I heard the <u>slithering</u>, I knew the snake was back.*

where it hit the rocks with a shower of sparks, and his leg was instantly torn with pain, as if a hundred needles had been driven into it. "Unnnngh!"

Now he screamed, with the pain and fear, and skittered on his backside up into the corner of the shelter, breathing through his mouth, straining to see, to hear.

The slithering moved again, he thought toward him at first, and terror took him, stopping his breath. He felt he could see a low dark form, a bulk in the darkness, a shadow that lived, but now it moved away, slithering and scraping it moved away and he saw or thought he saw it go out of the door opening.

He lay on his side for a moment, then pulled a <u>rasping</u> breath in and held it, listening for the attacker to return. When it was apparent that the shadow wasn't coming back he felt the calf of his leg, where the pain was centered and spreading to fill the whole leg.

▶ What attacked Brian?

His fingers <u>gingerly</u> touched a group of needles that had been driven through his pants and into the fleshy part of his calf. They were stiff and very sharp on the ends that stuck out, and he knew then what the attacker had been. A porcupine had stumbled into his shelter and when he had kicked it the thing had slapped him with its tail of quills.

He touched each quill carefully. The pain made it seem as if dozens of them had been slammed into his leg, but there were only eight, pinning the cloth against his skin. He leaned back against the wall for a minute. He couldn't leave them in, they had to come out, but just touching them made the pain more intense.

▶ How have things changed since Brian went to bed?

So fast, he thought. So fast things change. When he'd gone to sleep he had satisfaction and in just a moment it was all different. He grasped one of the quills, held his breath, and jerked. It sent pain signals to his brain in tight waves, but he grabbed another,

---

words for everyday use

rasp • ing (rasp' iŋ) *adj.*, grating, irritating. *The rusty gate made a <u>rasping</u> sound when Jan forced it open.*

gin • ger • ly (jin' jər lē) *adv.*, cautiously or carefully. *Raoul stepped <u>gingerly</u> on his sprained ankle.*

---

pulled it, then another quill. When he had pulled four of them he stopped for a moment. The pain had gone from being a pointed injury pain to spreading in a hot smear up his leg and it made him catch his breath.

Some of the quills were driven in deeper than others and they tore when they came out. He breathed deeply twice, let half of the breath out, and went back to work. Jerk, pause, jerk—and three more times before he lay back in the darkness, done. The pain filled his leg now, and with it came new waves of self-pity. Sitting alone in the dark, his leg aching, some mosquitos finding him again, he started crying. It was all too much, just too much, and he couldn't take it. Not the way it was.

I can't take it this way, alone with no fire and in the dark, and next time it might be something worse, maybe a bear, and it wouldn't be just quills in the leg, it would be worse. I can't do this, he thought, again and again. I can't. Brian pulled himself up until he was sitting upright back in the corner of the cave. He put his head down on his arms across his knees, with stiffness taking his left leg, and cried until he was cried out.

He did not know how long it took, but later he looked back on this time of crying in the corner of the dark cave and thought of it as when he learned the most important rule of survival, which was that feeling sorry for yourself didn't work. It wasn't just that it was wrong to do, or that it was considered incorrect. It was more than that—it didn't work. When he sat alone in the darkness and cried and was done, was all done with it, nothing had changed. His leg still hurt, it was still dark, he was still alone and the self-pity had accomplished nothing.

◀ *What important rule of survival did Brian learn?*

At last he slept again, but already his patterns were changing and the sleep was light, a resting doze more than a deep sleep, with small sounds awakening him twice in the rest of the night. In the last doze period before daylight, before he awakened finally with the morning light and the clouds of new mosquitos, he dreamed. This time it was not of his mother, not of the Secret, but of his father at first and then of his friend Terry.

In the initial segment of the dream his father was standing at the side of a living room looking at him and it was clear from his expression that he was trying to tell Brian something. His lips moved but there was no sound, not a whisper. He waved his hands at Brian, made gestures in front of his face as if he were scratching something, and he worked to make a word with his mouth but at first Brian could not see it. Then the lips made an *mmmmm* shape but no sound came. *Mmmmm—maaaa.* Brian could not hear it, could not understand it and he wanted to so badly; it was so important to understand his father, to know what he was saying. He was trying to help, trying so hard, and when Brian couldn't understand he looked cross, the way he did when Brian asked questions more than once, and he faded. Brian's father faded into a fog place Brian could not see and the dream was almost over, or seemed to be, when Terry came.

He was not gesturing to Brian but was sitting in the park at a bench looking at a barbecue pit and for a time nothing happened. Then he got up and poured some charcoal from a bag into the cooker, then some starter fluid, and he took a flick type of lighter and lit the fluid. When it was burning and the charcoal was at last getting hot he turned, noticing Brian for the first time in the dream. He turned and smiled and pointed to the fire as if to say, see, a fire.

▶ What do you think the dreams are trying to tell Brian?

But it meant nothing to Brian, except that he wished he had a fire. He saw a grocery sack on the table next to Terry. Brian thought it must contain hot dogs and chips and mustard and he could think only of the food. But Terry shook his head and pointed again to the fire, and twice more he pointed to the fire, made Brian see the flames, and Brian felt his frustration and anger rise and he thought all right, all right. I see the fire but so what? I don't have a fire. I know about fire; I know I need a fire.

I know that.

His eyes opened and there was light in the cave, a gray dim light of morning. He wiped his mouth and tried to move his leg, which had stiffened like wood. There was thirst, and hunger, and he ate some raspberries from the jacket. They had spoiled a bit,

seemed softer and mushier, but still had a rich sweetness. He crushed the berries against the roof of his
mouth with his tongue and drank the sweet juice as
it ran down his throat. A flash of metal caught his
eye and he saw his hatchet in the sand where he had
thrown it at the porcupine in the dark.

He scooched up, wincing a bit when he bent his
stiff leg, and crawled to where the hatchet lay. He
picked it up and examined it and saw a chip in the
top of the head.

The nick wasn't large, but the hatchet was important to him, was his only tool, and he should not
have thrown it. He should keep it in his hand, and
make a tool of some kind to help push an animal
away. Make a staff, he thought, or a lance, and save
the hatchet. Something came then, a thought as he
held the hatchet, something about the dream and his
father and Terry, but he couldn't pin it down.

"Ahhh . . ." He scrambled out and stood in the
morning sun and stretched his back muscles and his
sore leg. The hatchet was still in his hand, and as he
stretched and raised it over his head it caught the
first rays of the morning sun. The first faint light hit
the silver of the hatchet and it flashed a brilliant gold
in the light. Like fire. That is it, he thought. What
they were trying to tell me.

Fire. The hatchet was the key to it all. When he
threw the hatchet at the porcupine in the cave and
missed and hit the stone wall it had showered sparks,
a golden shower of sparks in the dark, as golden with
fire as the sun was now.

◀ *How will Brian
make fire?*

The hatchet was the answer. That's what his father
and Terry had been trying to tell him. Somehow he
could get fire from the hatchet. The sparks would
make fire.

Brian went back into the shelter and studied the
wall. It was some form of chalky granite, or a sandstone, but imbedded in it were large pieces of a

---

**words
for
everyday
use**   lance (lan[t]s) *n.,* spear or other long, sharp object. *The hunter thrust the lance into the
side of the animal.*

darker stone, a harder and darker stone. It only took him a moment to find where the hatchet had struck. The steel had nicked into the edge of one of the darker stone pieces. Brian turned the head backward so he would strike with the flat rear of the hatchet and hit the black rock gently. Too gently, and nothing happened. He struck harder, a glancing blow, and two or three weak sparks skipped off the rock and died immediately.

He swung harder, held the hatchet so it would hit a longer, sliding blow, and the black rock exploded in fire. Sparks flew so heavily that several of them skittered and jumped on the sand beneath the rock and he smiled and struck again and again.

There could be fire here, he thought. I will have a fire here, he thought, and struck again—I will have fire from the hatchet.

Respond to the Selection

What qualities do you think help a person survive? What qualities do you think you have that would help you survive if you were lost and stranded?

Investigate, Inquire, and Imagine

Recall: GATHER FACTS

1a. What three needs does Brian begin to take care of in chapter 5?

2a. What is the Secret?

3a. What does Brian say is the most important rule of survival?

Interpret: FIND MEANING

→ 1b. How successful is he in meeting each of these needs?

→ 2b. Why does Brian keep thinking about the Secret?

→ 3b. What other lessons has Brian started to learn?

Analyze: TAKE THINGS APART

4a. List the things Brian has to help him survive.

Synthesize: BRING THINGS TOGETHER

→ 4b. Which of these things do you think is most important? Why?

Evaluate: MAKE JUDGMENTS

5a. Assess how Brian's experience is different from what is typically portrayed in adventure or survival movies.

Extend: CONNECT IDEAS

→ 5b. What things have you read or seen on TV or in the movies that might help you survive in a situation similar to Brian's?

Understanding Literature

CHARACTER AND CHARACTERIZATION. A **character** is a person or animal who takes part in the action of a literary work. **Characterization** is the act of creating or describing a character. Writers create characters using three major techniques: showing what characters say, do, or think; showing what other characters say or think about them; and by describing the physical features, dress, and personality of the character. On your own paper, create a chart like the one below. Complete the chart with details about Brian. Then describe Brian in your own words.

What Brian Says, Does, or Thinks	Description of Brian's Features, Dress, and Personality

MOTIVATION. A **motivation** is a force that moves a character to think, feel, or behave in a certain way. What motivates Brian to set up a shelter, eat the gut cherries, and try to make fire?

SETTING. The setting is the time and place in which a literary work takes place. Most of the novel takes place near a lake where the plane crashed. Describe this setting in more detail. What time of year is it, and what is the place like?

Chapter 9

Brian found it was a long way from sparks to fire.

Clearly there had to be something for the sparks to ignite, some kind of tinder or kindling[1]—but what? He brought some dried grass in, tapped sparks into it and watched them die. He tried small twigs, breaking them into little pieces, but that was worse than the grass. Then he tried a combination of the two, grass and twigs.

Nothing. He had no trouble getting sparks, but the tiny bits of hot stone or metal—he couldn't tell which they were—just sputtered and died.

◀ What trouble does Brian have trying to light a fire?

He settled back on his haunches[2] in exasperation, looking at the pitiful clump of grass and twigs.

He needed something finer, something soft and fine and fluffy to catch the bits of fire.

Shredded paper would be nice, but he had no paper.

"So close," he said aloud, "so close . . ."

He put the hatchet back in his belt and went out of the shelter, limping on his sore leg. There had to be something, had to be. Man had made fire. There had been fire for thousands, millions of years. There had to be a way. He dug in his pockets and found the twenty-dollar bill in his wallet. Paper. Worthless paper out here. But if he could get a fire going . . .

---

1. **tinder or kindling.** Materials, such as dried grass or small sticks, used to start a fire. Tinder is generally smaller or finer than kindling.
2. **on his haunches.** In a squatting position

He ripped the twenty into tiny pieces, made a pile of pieces, and hit sparks into them. Nothing happened. They just wouldn't take the sparks. But there had to be a way—some way to do it.

Not twenty feet to his right, leaning out over the water were birches and he stood looking at them for a full half-minute before they registered on his mind. They were a beautiful white with bark like clean, slightly speckled paper.

Paper.

He moved to the trees. Where the bark was peeling from the trunks it lifted in tiny <u>tendrils</u>, almost fluffs. Brian plucked some of them loose, rolled them in his fingers. They seemed flammable, dry and nearly powdery. He pulled and twisted bits off the trees, packing them in one hand while he picked them with the other, picking and gathering until he had a wad close to the size of a baseball.

Then he went back into the shelter and arranged the ball of birchbark peelings at the base of the black rock. As an afterthought he threw in the remains of the twenty-dollar bill. He struck and a stream of sparks fell into the bark and quickly died. But this time one spark fell on one small hair of dry bark— almost a thread of bark—and seemed to glow a bit brighter before it died.

The material had to be finer. There had to be a soft and incredibly fine nest for the sparks.

I must make a home for the sparks, he thought. A perfect home or they won't stay, they won't make fire.

He started ripping the bark, using his fingernails at first, and when that didn't work he used the sharp edge of the hatchet, cutting the bark in thin slivers, hairs so fine they were almost not there. It was <u>painstaking</u> work, slow work, and he stayed with it for over two hours. Twice he stopped for a handful of berries and once to go to the lake for a drink. Then

▶ What does Brian notice around him that will help him build a fire?

---

words for everyday use

ten • dril (ten' drəl) n., slender bit that coils or curls. *Kira wore her hair up, except for a few <u>tendrils</u> that curled down the back of her neck.*

pain • stak • ing (pān' stā kiŋ) adj., taking care and effort. *Making sure that no paint touched the windowsill was <u>painstaking</u> work.*

back to work, the sun on his back, until at last he had a ball of fluff as big as a grapefruit—dry birchbark fluff.

He positioned his spark nest—as he thought of it—at the base of the rock, used his thumb to make a small depression in the middle, and slammed the back of the hatchet down across the black rock. A cloud of sparks rained down, most of them missing the nest, but some, perhaps thirty or so, hit in the depression and of those six or seven found fuel and grew, smoldered and caused the bark to take on the red glow.

Then they went out.

Close—he was close. He repositioned the nest, made a new and smaller dent with his thumb, and struck again.

More sparks, a slight glow, then nothing.

It's me, he thought. I'm doing something wrong. I do not know this—a cave dweller would have had a fire by now, a Cro-Magnon man[3] would have a fire by now—but I don't know this. I don't know how to make a fire.

Maybe not enough sparks. He settled the nest in place once more and hit the rock with a series of blows, as fast as he could. The sparks poured like a golden waterfall. At first they seemed to take, there were several, many sparks that found life and took briefly, but they all died.

Starved.

He leaned back. They are like me. They are starving. It wasn't quantity, there were plenty of sparks, but they needed more.

I would kill, he thought suddenly, for a book of matches. Just one book. Just one match. I would kill.

What makes fire? He thought back to school. To all those science classes. Had he ever learned what made a fire? Did a teacher ever stand up there and say, "This is what makes a fire . . ."

He shook his head, tried to focus his thoughts. What did it take? You have to have fuel, he thought—and he had that. The bark was fuel. Oxygen—there had to be air.

◀ *What is Brian doing wrong? What does he need to do to make fire?*

---

3. **Cro-Magnon man.** Early race of humans

He needed to add air. He had to fan on it, blow on it.

He made the nest ready again, held the hatchet backward, tensed, and struck four quick blows. Sparks came down and he leaned forward as fast as he could and blew.

Too hard. There was a bright, almost intense glow, then it was gone. He had blown it out.

Another set of strikes, more sparks. He leaned and blew, but gently this time, holding back and aiming the stream of air from his mouth to hit the brightest spot. Five or six sparks had fallen in a tight mass of bark hair and Brian centered his efforts there.

The sparks grew with his gentle breath. The red glow moved from the sparks themselves into the bark, moved and grew and became worms, glowing red worms that crawled up the bark hairs and caught other threads of bark and grew until there was a pocket of red as big as a quarter, a glowing red coal of heat.

And when he ran out of breath and paused to inhale, the red ball suddenly burst into flame.

"Fire!" He yelled. "I've got fire! I've got it, I've got it, I've got it . . ."

But the flames were thick and oily and burning fast, consuming the ball of bark as fast as if it were gasoline. He had to feed the flames, keep them going. Working as fast as he could he carefully placed the dried grass and wood pieces he had tried at first on top of the bark and was <u>gratified</u> to see them take.

But they would go fast. He needed more, and more. He could not let the flames go out.

He ran from the shelter to the pines and started breaking off the low, dead small limbs. These he threw in the shelter, went back for more, threw those in, and squatted to break and feed the hungry flames. When the small wood was going well he went out and found larger wood and did not relax until that

---

words for everyday use   **grat • i • fy** (grat' ə fī) v., satisfy, please. *Birungi was <u>gratified</u> that Louis acknowledged her efforts.*

was going. Then he leaned back against the wood brace of his door opening and smiled.

I have a friend, he thought—I have a friend now. A hungry friend, but a good one. I have a friend named fire.

◀ Why does Brian think of fire as a hungry friend?

"Hello, fire . . ."

The curve of the rock back made an almost perfect drawing flue that carried the smoke up through the cracks of the roof but held the heat. If he kept the fire small it would be perfect and would keep anything like the porcupine from coming through the door again.

A friend and a guard, he thought.

So much from a little spark. A friend and a guard from a tiny spark.

He looked around and wished he had somebody to tell this thing, to show this thing he had done. But there was nobody.

Nothing but the trees and the sun and the breeze and the lake.

Nobody.

And he thought, rolling thoughts, with the smoke curling up over his head and the smile still half on his face he thought: I wonder what they're doing now.

I wonder what my father is doing now.

I wonder what my mother is doing now.

I wonder if she is with him.

Chapter 10

He could not at first leave the fire.

▶ Why can Brian not leave the fire at first?

It was so precious to him, so close and sweet a thing, the yellow and red flames brightening the dark interior of the shelter, the happy crackle of the dry wood as it burned, that he could not leave it. He went to the trees and brought in as many dead limbs as he could chop off and carry, and when he had a large pile of them he sat near the fire—though it was getting into the warm middle part of the day and he was hot—and broke them in small pieces and fed the fire.

I will not let you go out, he said to himself, to the flames—not ever. And so he sat through a long part of the day, keeping the flames even, eating from his stock of raspberries, leaving to drink from the lake when he was thirsty. In the afternoon, toward evening, with his face smoke smeared and his skin red from the heat, he finally began to think ahead to what he needed to do.

He would need a large woodpile to get through the night. It would be almost impossible to find wood in the dark so he had to have it all in and cut and stacked before the sun went down.

Brian made certain the fire was banked[1] with new wood, then went out of the shelter and searched for a good fuel supply. Up the hill from the campsite the

---

1. **banked.** Cover a fire with fuel in such a way as to keep it in an inactive state

same windstorm that left him a place to land the plane—had that only been three, four days ago?—had dropped three large white pines across each other. They were dead now, dry and filled with weathered dry dead limbs—enough for many days. He chopped and broke and carried wood back to the camp, stacking the pieces under the overhang until he had what he thought to be an enormous pile, as high as his head and six feet across the base. Between trips he added small pieces to the fire to keep it going and on one of the trips to get wood he noticed an added advantage of the fire. When he was in the shade of the trees breaking limbs the mosquitos swarmed on him, as usual, but when he came to the fire, or just near the shelter where the smoke <u>eddied</u> and swirled, the insects were gone.

◀ What two other benefits of fire does Brian notice?

It was a wonderful discovery. The mosquitos had nearly driven him mad and the thought of being rid of them lifted his spirits. On another trip he looked back and saw the smoke curling up through the trees and realized, for the first time, that he now had the means to make a signal. He could carry a burning stick and build a signal fire on top of the rock, make clouds of smoke and perhaps attract attention.

Which meant more wood. And still more wood. There did not seem to be an end to the wood he would need and he spent all the rest of the afternoon into dusk making wood trips.

At dark he settled in again for the night, next to the fire with the stack of short pieces ready to put on, and he ate the rest of the raspberries. During all the work of the day his leg had loosened but it still ached a bit, and he rubbed it and watched the fire and thought for the first time since the crash that he might be getting a handle on things, might be starting to do something other than just sit.

He was out of food, but he could look tomorrow and he could build a signal fire tomorrow and get more wood tomorrow . . .

words for everyday use
ed • dy (ed′ ē) v., move like a whirlpool. *The toy boat swirled as the water <u>eddied</u> down the drain.*

The fire cut the night coolness and settled him back into sleep, thinking of tomorrow.

He slept hard and wasn't sure what awakened him but his eyes came open and he stared into the darkness. The fire had burned down and looked out but he stirred with a piece of wood and found a bed of coals still glowing hot and red. With small pieces of wood and careful blowing he soon had a blaze going again.

▶ Why does Brian want to regulate his sleep?

It had been close. He had to be sure to try and sleep in short intervals so he could keep the fire going, and he tried to think of a way to <u>regulate</u> his sleep but it made him sleepy to think about it and he was just going under again when he heard the sound outside.

It was not unlike the sound of the porcupine, something slithering and being dragged across the sand, but when he looked out the door opening it was too dark to see anything.

Whatever it was it stopped making that sound in a few moments and he thought he heard something sloshing into the water at the shoreline, but he had the fire now and plenty of wood so he wasn't as worried as he had been the night before.

He dozed, slept for a time, awakened again just at dawn-gray light, and added wood to the still-smoking fire before standing outside and stretching. Standing with his arms stretched over his head and the tight knot of hunger in his stomach, he looked toward the lake and saw the tracks.

They were strange, a main center line up from the lake in the sand with claw marks to the side leading to a small pile of sand, then going back down to the water.

He walked over and squatted near them, studied them, tried to make sense of them.

Whatever had made the tracks had some kind of flat dragging bottom in the middle and was apparently pushed along by the legs that stuck out to the side.

words for everyday use

reg • u • late (reg' yə lāt) v., control, order. *You <u>regulate</u> your eating habits by slowing down and eating less.*

Up from the water to a small pile of sand, then back down into the water. Some animal. Some kind of water animal that came up to the sand to . . . to do what?

To do something with the sand, to play and make a pile in the sand?

He smiled. City boy, he thought. Oh, you city boy with your city ways—he made a mirror in his mind, a mirror of himself, and saw how he must look. City boy with your city ways sitting in the sand trying to read the tracks and not knowing, not understanding. Why would anything wild come up from the water to play in the sand? Not that way, animals weren't that way. They didn't waste time that way.

◄ What animal came up from the water? Why?

It had come up from the water for a reason, a good reason, and he must try to understand the reason, he must change to fully understand the reason himself or he would not make it.

It had come up from the water for a reason, and the reason, he thought, squatting, the reason had to do with the pile of sand.

He brushed the top off gently with his hand but found only damp sand. Still, there must be a reason and he carefully kept scraping and digging until, about four inches down, he suddenly came into a small chamber in the cool-damp sand and there lay eggs, many eggs, almost perfectly round eggs the size of table tennis balls, and he laughed then because he knew.

It had been a turtle. He had seen a show on television about sea turtles that came up onto beaches and laid their eggs in the sand. There must be freshwater lake turtles that did the same. Maybe snapping turtles. He had heard of snapping turtles. They became fairly large, he thought. It must have been a snapper that came up in the night when he heard the noise that awakened him; she must have come then and laid the eggs.

Food.

More than eggs, more than knowledge, more than anything this was food. His stomach tightened and rolled and made noise as he looked at the eggs, as if his stomach belonged to somebody else or had seen the eggs with its own eyes and was demanding food. The hunger, always there, had been somewhat controlled and <u>dormant</u> when there was nothing to eat but with the eggs came the scream to eat. His whole body craved food with such an intensity that it quickened his breath.

He reached into the nest and pulled the eggs out one at a time. There were seventeen of them, each as round as a ball, and white. They had leathery shells that gave instead of breaking when he squeezed them.

When he had them heaped on the sand in a pyramid—he had never felt so rich somehow—he suddenly realized that he did not know how to eat them.

He had a fire but no way to cook them, no container, and he had never thought of eating a raw egg. He had an uncle named Carter, his father's brother, who always put an egg in a glass of milk and drank it in the morning. Brian had watched him do it once, just once, and when the runny part of the white left the glass and went into his uncle's mouth and down the throat in a single gulp Brian almost lost everything he had ever eaten.

Still, he thought. Still. As his stomach moved toward his backbone he became less and less fussy. Some natives in the world ate grasshoppers and ants and if they could do that he could get a raw egg down.

He picked one up and tried to break the shell and found it surprisingly tough. Finally, using the hatchet he sharpened a stick and poked a hole in the egg. He widened the hole with his finger and looked inside. Just an egg. It had a dark yellow yolk and not so much white as he thought there would be.

Just an egg.

Food.

Just an egg he had to eat.

Raw.

He looked out across the lake and brought the egg to his mouth and closed his eyes and sucked and

▶ How does Brian feel about eating the eggs?

words for everyday use

dor • mant (dôr′ mənt) *adj.,* asleep or inactive. *Many animals are in <u>dormant</u> states during the heat of the day.*

squeezed the egg at the same time and swallowed as fast as he could.

"Ecch . . ."

It had a greasy, almost oily taste, but it was still an egg. His throat tried to throw it back up, his whole body seemed to <u>convulse</u> with it, but his stomach took it, held it, and demanded more.

The second egg was easier, and by the third one he had no trouble at all—it just slid down. He ate six of them, could have easily eaten all of them and not been full, but a part of him said to hold back, save the rest.

He could not now believe the hunger. The eggs had awakened it fully, roaringly, so that it tore at him. After the sixth egg he ripped the shell open and licked the inside clean, then went back and ripped the other five open and licked them out as well and wondered if he could eat the shells. There must be some food value in them. But when he tried they were too leathery to chew and he couldn't get them down.

He stood away from the eggs for a moment, literally stood and turned away so that he could not see them. If he looked at them he would have to eat more.

He would store them in the shelter and eat only one a day. He fought the hunger down again, controlled it. He would take them now and store them and save them and eat one a day, and he realized as he thought it that he had forgotten that *they* might come. The searchers. Surely, they would come before he could eat all the eggs at one a day.

He had forgotten to think about them and that wasn't good. He had to keep thinking of them because if he forgot them and did not think of them they might forget about him.

And he had to keep hoping.

He had to keep hoping.

◄ *What did Brian forget for a moment? Why is it important to him to remember this?*

words for everyday use

con • vulse (kən vuls′) v., shake violently as with spasm. *The angry baby <u>convulsed</u> and cried, then suddenly quieted and grew still.*

Chapter 11

There were these things to do.

He transferred all the eggs from the small beach into the shelter, reburying them near his sleeping area. It took all his will to keep from eating another one as he moved them, but he got it done and when they were out of sight again it was easier. He added wood to the fire and cleaned up the camp area.

A good laugh, that—cleaning the camp. All he did was shake out his windbreaker and hang it in the sun to dry the berry juice that had soaked in, and smooth the sand where he slept.

▶ How does staying busy help Brian?

But it was a mental thing. He had gotten depressed thinking about how they hadn't found him yet, and when he was busy and had something to do the depression seemed to leave.

So there were things to do.

With the camp squared away he brought in more wood. He had decided to always have enough on hand for three days and after spending one night with the fire for a friend he knew what a staggering amount of wood it would take. He worked all through the morning at the wood, breaking down dead limbs and breaking or chopping them in smaller pieces, storing them neatly beneath the overhang. He stopped once to take a drink at the lake and in his reflection he saw that the swelling on his head was nearly gone. There was no pain there so he assumed that had taken care of itself. His leg was also back to normal, although he had a small pattern of holes—roughly star-shaped—where the quills had nailed him, and while he was standing at the lake shore taking stock he noticed that his body was changing.

He had never been fat, but he had been slightly heavy with a little extra weight just above his belt at the sides.

◀ How has Brian changed?

This was completely gone and his stomach had caved in to the hunger and the sun had cooked him past burning so he was tanning, and with the smoke from the fire his face was starting to look like leather. But perhaps more than his body was the change in his mind, or in the way he was—was becoming.

I am not the same, he thought. I see, I hear differently. He did not know when the change started, but it was there; when a sound came to him now he didn't just hear it but would know the sound. He would swing and look at it—a breaking twig, a movement of air—and know the sound as if he somehow could move his mind back down the wave of sound to the source.

He could know what the sound was before he quite realized he had heard it. And when he saw something—a bird moving a wing inside a bush or a ripple on the water—he would truly see that thing, not just notice it as he used to notice things in the city. He would see all parts of it; see the whole wing, the feathers, see the color of the feathers, see the bush, and the size and shape and color of its leaves. He would see the way the light moved with the ripples on the water and see that the wind made the ripples and which way that wind had to blow to make the ripples move in that certain way.

None of that used to be in Brian and now it was a part of him, a changed part of him, a grown part of him, and the two things, his mind and his body, had come together as well, had made a connection with each other that he didn't quite understand. When his ears heard a sound or his eyes saw a sight his mind took control of his body. Without his thinking, he moved to face the sound or sight, moved to make ready for it, to deal with it.

There were these things to do.

When the wood was done he decided to get a signal fire ready. He moved to the top of the rock ridge that comprised the <u>bluff</u> over his shelter and was pleased to find a large, flat stone area.

More wood, he thought, moaning inwardly. He went back to the fallen trees and found more dead limbs, carrying them up on the rock until he had enough for a bonfire. Initially he had thought of making a signal fire every day but he couldn't—he would never be able to keep the wood supply going. So while he was working he decided to have the fire ready and if he heard an engine, or even thought he heard a plane engine, he would run up with a burning limb and set off the signal fire.

▶ Why won't Brian keep a signal fire going all of the time?

Things to do.

At the last trip to the top of the stone bluff with wood he stopped, sat on the point overlooking the lake, and rested. The lake lay before him, twenty or so feet below, and he had not seen it this way since he had come in with the plane. Remembering the crash he had a moment of fear, a breath-tightening little rip of terror, but it passed and he was quickly caught up in the beauty of the scenery.

It was so incredibly beautiful that it was almost unreal. From his height he could see not just the lake but across part of the forest, a green carpet, and it was full of life. Birds, insects—there was a constant hum and song. At the other end of the bottom of the L there was another large rock sticking out over the water and on top of the rock a snaggly pine had somehow found food and grown, bent and gnarled.

▶ How does watching the bird help Brian?

Sitting on one limb was a blue bird with a crest and sharp beak, a kingfisher—he thought of a picture he had seen once—which left the branch while he watched and dove into the water. It emerged a split part of a second later. In its mouth was a small fish,

---

words for everyday use

bluff (bluf) *n.,* steep bank. *One side of the river is a high <u>bluff</u>; the other is a beach that rises gradually.*

wiggling silver in the sun. It took the fish to a limb, juggled it twice, and swallowed it whole.

Fish.

Of course, he thought. There were fish in the lake and they were food. And if a bird could do it . . .

He scrambled down the side of the bluff and trotted to the edge of the lake, looking down into the water. Somehow it had never occurred to him to look *inside* the water—only at the surface. The sun was flashing back up into his eyes and he moved off to the side and took his shoes off and waded out fifteen feet. Then he turned and stood still, with the sun at his back, and studied the water again.

It was, he saw after a moment, literally packed with life. Small fish swam everywhere, some narrow and long, some round, most of them three or four inches long, some a bit larger and many smaller. There was a patch of mud off to the side, leading into deeper water, and he could see old clam shells there, so there must be clams. As he watched, a crayfish, looking like a tiny lobster, left one of the empty clam shells and went to another looking for something to eat, digging with its claws.

While he stood some of the small, roundish fish came quite close to his legs and he tensed, got ready, and made a wild stab at grabbing one of them. They exploded away in a hundred flicks of quick light, so fast that he had no hope of catching them that way. But they soon came back, seemed to be curious about him, and as he walked from the water he tried to think of a way to use that curiosity to catch them.

He had no hooks or string but if he could somehow lure them into the shallows—and make a spear, a small fish spear—he might be able to strike fast enough to get one.

◀ How does Brian plan to catch a fish?

He would have to find the right kind of wood, slim and straight—he had seen some willows up along the lake that might work—and he could use the hatchet to sharpen it and shape it while he was sitting by the fire tonight. And that brought up the fire, which he had to feed again. He looked at the sun and saw it was getting late in the afternoon, and when he thought of how late it was he thought that he ought to reward all his work with another egg and that made him think that some kind of dessert would be nice—he smiled when he thought of dessert, so fancy—and he wondered if he should move up the lake and see if he could find some raspberries after he banked the fire and while he was looking for the right wood for a spear. Spearwood, he thought, and it all rolled together, just rolled together and rolled over him . . .

There were these things to do.

Chapter 12

The fish spear didn't work.

He stood in the shallows and waited, again and again. The small fish came closer and closer and he lunged time after time but was always too slow. He tried throwing it, jabbing it, everything but <u>flailing</u> with it, and it didn't work. The fish were just too fast.

He had been so sure, so absolutely certain that it would work the night before. Sitting by the fire he had taken the willow and carefully peeled the bark until he had a straight staff about six feet long and just under an inch thick at the base, the thickest end.

Then, propping the hatchet in a crack in the rock wall, he had pulled the head of his spear against it, carving a thin piece off each time, until the thick end tapered down to a needle point. Still not satisfied— he could not imagine hitting one of the fish with a single point—he carefully used the hatchet to split the point up the middle for eight or ten inches and jammed a piece of wood up into the split to make a two-prong spear with the points about two inches apart. It was crude, but it looked effective and seemed to have good balance when he stood outside the shelter and <u>hefted</u> the spear.

words for everyday use

flail (flā[ə]l) v., beat or swing wildly. *Quint <u>flailed</u> about in the water, pretending that he did not know how to swim.*

heft (heft) v., to lift or throw. *After workers <u>hefted</u> heavy sandbags onto the lawn, the flood waters stopped creeping toward the house.*

▶ Why is the spear so important to Brian?

He had worked on the fish spear until it had become more than just a tool. He'd spent hours and hours on it, and now it didn't work. He moved into the shallows and stood and the fish came to him. Just as before they swarmed around his legs, some of them almost six inches long, but no matter how he tried they were too fast. At first he tried throwing it but that had no chance. As soon as he brought his arm back—well before he threw—the movement frightened them. Next he tried lunging at them, having the spear ready just above the water and thrusting with it. Finally he actually put the spear in the water and waited until the fish were right in front of it, but still somehow he <u>telegraphed</u> his motion before he thrust and they saw it and flashed away.

He needed something to spring the spear forward, some way to make it move faster than the fish—some motive force. A string that snapped—or a bow. A bow and arrow. A thin, long arrow with the point in the water and the bow pulled back so that all he had to do was release the arrow . . . yes. That was it.

▶ What does Brian learn about invention?

He had to "invent" the bow and arrow—he almost laughed as he moved out of the water and put his shoes on. The morning sun was getting hot and he took his shirt off. Maybe that was how it really happened, way back when—some primitive man tried to spear fish and it didn't work and he "invented" the bow and arrow. Maybe it was always that way, discoveries happened because they needed to happen.

He had not eaten anything yet this morning so he took a moment to dig up the eggs and eat one. Then he reburied them, banked the fire with a couple of thicker pieces of wood, settled the hatchet on his belt and took the spear in his right hand and set off up the lake to find wood to make a bow. He went without a shirt but something about the wood smoke smell on him kept the insects from bothering him as he walked to the berry patch. The raspberries were

---

words for everyday use   **tel • e • graph** (tel' ə graf) v., to make known by signs in advance. *If you <u>telegraph</u> the pass, the other team will steal the ball.*

starting to become overripe, just in two days, and he would have to pick as many as possible after he found the wood but he did take a little time now to pick a few and eat them. They were full and sweet and when he picked one, two others would fall off the limbs into the grass and soon his hands and cheeks were covered with red berry juice and he was full. That surprised him—being full.

He hadn't thought he would ever be full again, knew only the hunger, and here he was full. One turtle egg and a few handfuls of berries and he felt full. He looked down at his stomach and saw that it was still caved in—did not bulge out as it would have with two hamburgers and a freezy slush. It must have shrunk. And there was still hunger there, but not like it was—not tearing at him. This was hunger that he knew would be there always, even when he had food—a hunger that made him look for things, see things. A hunger to make him hunt.

◀ What new hunger does Brian have?

He swung his eyes across the berries to make sure the bear wasn't there, at his back, then he moved down to the lake. The spear went out before him automatically, moving the brush away from his face as he walked, and when he came to the water's edge he swung left. Not sure what he was looking for, not knowing what wood might be best for a bow—he had never made a bow, never shot a bow in his life—but it seemed that it would be along the lake, near the water.

He saw some young birch, and they were springy, but they lacked snap somehow, as did the willows. Not enough whip-back.

Halfway up the lake, just as he started to step over a log, he was absolutely terrified by an explosion under his feet. Something like a feathered bomb blew up and away in flurry of leaves and thunder. It frightened him so badly that he fell back and down and then it was gone, leaving only an image in his mind.

A bird, it had been, about the size of a very small chicken only with a fantail and stubby wings that slammed against its body and made loud noise. Noise there and gone. He got up and brushed himself off. The bird had been speckled, brown and gray, and

◀ What is Brian's first thought when he almost steps on the bird?

it must not be very smart because Brian's foot had been nearly on it before it flew. Half a second more and he would have stepped on it.

And caught it, he thought, and eaten it. He might be able to catch one, or spear one. Maybe, he thought, maybe it tasted like chicken. Maybe he could catch one or spear one and it probably did taste just like chicken. Just like chicken when his mother baked it in the oven with garlic and salt and it turned golden brown and crackled. . . .

He shook his head to drive the picture out and moved down to the shore. There was a tree there with long branches that seemed straight and when he pulled on one of them and let go it had an almost vicious snap to it. He picked one of the limbs that seemed right and began chopping where the limb joined the tree.

The wood was hard and he didn't want to cause it to split so he took his time, took small chips and concentrated so hard that at first he didn't hear it.

▶ What sound does Brian hear? What does this sound mean to him?

A persistent whine, like the insects only more steady with an edge of a roar to it, was in his ears and he chopped and cut and was thinking of a bow, how he would make a bow, how it would be when he shaped it with the hatchet and still the sound did not cut through until the limb was nearly off the tree and the whine was inside his head and he knew it then.

A plane! It was a motor, far off but seeming to get louder. They were coming for him!

He threw down the limb and his spear and, holding the hatchet, he started to run for camp. He had to get fire up on the bluff and signal them, get fire and smoke up. He put all of his life into his legs, jumped logs and moved through brush like a light ghost, swiveling and running, his lungs filling and blowing and now the sound was louder, coming in his direction.

If not right at him, at least closer. He could see it all in his mind now, the picture, the way it would be. He would get the fire going and the plane would see the smoke and circle, circle once, then again, and waggle its wings. It would be a float plane and it would land on the water and come across the lake and the pilot would be amazed that he was alive after all these days.

All this he saw as he ran for the camp and the fire. They would take him from here and this night, this very night, he would sit with his father and eat and tell him all the things. He could see it now. Oh, yes, all as he ran in the sun, his legs liquid springs. He got to the camp still hearing the whine of the engine, and one stick of wood still had good flame.

He dove inside and grabbed the wood and ran around the edge of the ridge, scrambled up like a cat and blew and nearly had the flame feeding, growing, when the sound moved away.

It was abrupt, as if the plane had turned. He shielded the sun from his eyes and tried to see it, tried to make the plane become real in his eyes. But the trees were so high, so thick, and now the sound was still fainter. He kneeled again to the flames and blew and added grass and chips and the flames fed and grew and in moments he had a bonfire as high as his head but the sound was gone now.

Look back, he thought. Look back and see the smoke now and turn, please turn.

"Look back," he whispered, feeling all the pictures fade, seeing his father's face fade like the sound, like lost dreams, like an end to hope. Oh, turn now and come back, look back and see the smoke and turn for me. . . .

But it kept moving away until he could not hear it even in his imagination, in his soul. Gone. He stood on the bluff over the lake, his face cooking in the roaring bonfire, watching the clouds of ash and smoke going into the sky and thought—no, more than thought—he knew then that he would not get out of this place. Not now, not ever.

◀ What thought does Brian have when the plane turns away?

That had been a search plane. He was sure of it. That must have been them and they had come as far off to the side of the flight plan as they thought they would have to come and then turned back. They did not see his smoke, did not hear the cry from his mind.

They would not return. He would never leave now, never get out of here. He went down to his knees and felt the tears start, cutting through the smoke and ash on his face, silently falling onto the stone.

Gone, he thought finally, it was all gone. All silly and gone. No bows, no spears, or fish or berries, it was all silly anyway, all just a game. He could do a day, but not forever—he could not make it if they did not come for him someday.

He could not play the game without hope; could not play the game without a dream. They had taken it all away from him now, they had turned away from him and there was nothing for him now. The plane gone, his family gone, all of it gone. They would not come. He was alone and there was nothing for him.

▶ How does Brian feel when he realizes the plane did not see him?

Respond to the Selection

Imagine you are Brian, and you see that the plane is not coming back. How would you feel? What would you do? What do you think will happen to Brian next?

Investigate, Inquire, and Imagine

Recall: GATHER FACTS

1a. What steps does Brian take to make fire?

2a. What is Brian's first thought when he sees the turtle tracks? Why did the turtle come up from the water?

3a. What does Brian have to "invent" in order to catch fish?

Interpret: FIND MEANING

1b. Why is the fire so important to Brian?

2b. Why is it important that Brian understand why the turtle came up from the water?

3b. What does Brian learn about inventions?

Analyze: TAKE THINGS APART

4a. Chapter 11 begins, "There were these things to do." What things does Brian have to do?

Synthesize: BRING THINGS TOGETHER

4b. Why are all these activities important to Brian?

Evaluate: MAKE JUDGMENTS

5a. Judge Brian's chances for survival now that the search planes seem to have missed him. Why are things different now?

Extend: CONNECT IDEAS

5b. In what other situations do you think hope can help a person? Give an example from your own life of a time when hope helped you.

Understanding Literature

CENTRAL CONFLICT. A **central conflict** is the main struggle between two people or things in a literary work. Conflicts in literary works are often human versus human, human versus nature, or human versus self. What two conflicts does Brian face? Which do you think is the central conflict? Why?

CRISIS. The **crisis**, or **turning point,** is the point in a plot when something happens to determine the future course of events and the eventual fate of the main character. Why does the airplane noise in the distance mark the crisis in the story?

Chapter 13

Brian stood at the end of the long part of the L of the lake and watched the water, smelled the water, listened to the water, was the water.

A fish moved and his eyes jerked sideways to see the ripples but he did not move any other part of his body and did not raise the bow or reach into his belt pouch for a fish arrow. It was not the right kind of fish, not a food fish.

The food fish stayed close in, in the shallows, and did not roll that way but made quicker movements, small movements, food movements. The large fish rolled and stayed deep and could not be taken. But it didn't matter. This day, this morning, he was not looking for fish. Fish was light meat and he was sick of them.

He was looking for one of the foolish birds—he called them foolbirds—and there was a flock that lived near the end of the long part of the lake. But something he did not understand had stopped him and he stood, breathing gently through his mouth to keep silent, letting his eyes and ears go out and do the work for him.

It had happened before this way, something had come into him from outside to warn him and he had stopped. Once it had been the bear again. He had been taking the last of the raspberries and something came inside and stopped him, and when he

▶ What is Brian's attitude toward the fish?

▶ How did Brian's senses help him once before?

looked where his ears said to look there was a female bear with cubs.

Had he taken two more steps he would have come between the mother and her cubs and that was a bad place to be. As it was the mother had stood and faced him and made a sound, a low sound in her throat to threaten and warn him. He paid attention to the feeling now and he stood and waited, patiently, knowing he was right and that something would come.

Turn, smell, listen, feel and then a sound, a small sound, and he looked up and away from the lake and saw the wolf. It was halfway up the hill from the lake, standing with its head and shoulders sticking out into a small opening, looking down on him with wide yellow eyes. He had never seen a wolf and the size threw him—not as big as a bear but somehow seeming that large. The wolf claimed all that was below him as his own, took Brian as his own.

Brian looked back and for a moment felt afraid because the wolf was so . . . so right. He knew Brian, knew him and owned him and chose not to do anything to him. But the fear moved then, moved away, and Brian knew the wolf for what it was—another part of the woods, another part of all of it. Brian relaxed the tension on the spear in his hand, settled the bow in his other hand from where it had started to come up. He knew the wolf now, as the wolf knew him, and he nodded to it, nodded and smiled.

The wolf watched him for another time, another part of his life, then it turned and walked effortlessly up the hill and as it came out of the brush it was followed by three other wolves, all equally large and gray and beautiful, all looking down on him as they trotted past and away and Brian nodded to each of them.

He was not the same now—the Brian that stood and watched the wolves move away and nodded to them was completely changed. Time had come, time that he measured but didn't care about; time had come into his life and moved out and left him different.

In measured time forty-seven days had passed since the crash. Forty-two days, he thought, since he had died and been born as the new Brian.

◄ How long has it been since the crash? How long since the plane passed him?

When the plane had come and gone it had put him down, gutted him and dropped him and left him with nothing. The rest of that first day he had gone down and down until dark. He had let the fire go out, had forgotten to eat even an egg, had let his brain take him down to where he was done, where he wanted to be done and done.

To where he wanted to die. He had settled into the gray funk deeper and still deeper until finally, in the dark, he had gone up on the ridge and taken the hatchet and tried to end it by cutting himself.

Madness. A hissing madness that took his brain. There had been nothing for him then and he tried to become nothing but the cutting had been hard to do, impossible to do, and he had at last fallen to his side, wishing for death, wishing for an end, and slept only didn't sleep.

With his eyes closed and his mind open he lay on the rock through the night, lay and hated and wished for it to end and thought the word *Clouddown, Clouddown* through that awful night. Over and over the word, wanting all his clouds to come down, but in the morning he was still there.

Still there on his side and the sun came up and when he opened his eyes he saw the cuts on his arm, the dry blood turning black; he saw the blood and hated the blood, hated what he had done to himself when he was the old Brian and was weak, and two things came into his mind—two true things.

He was not the same. The plane passing changed him, the disappointment cut him down and made him new. He was not the same and would never be again like he had been. That was one of the true things, the new things. And the other one was that he would not die, he would not let death in again.

He was new.

Of course he had made a lot of mistakes. He smiled now, walking up the lake shore after the wolves were gone, thinking of the early mistakes; the mistakes that came before he realized that he had to find new ways to be what he had become.

He had made new fire, which he now kept going using partially rotten wood because the punky wood

▶ What did Brian try to do at his low point?

▶ What two things are true of the new Brian?

would smolder for many hours and still come back with fire. But that had been the extent of doing things right for a while. His first bow was a disaster that almost blinded him.

He had sat a whole night and shaped the limbs carefully until the bow looked beautiful. Then he had spent two days making arrows. The shafts were willow, straight and with the bark peeled, and he fire-hardened the points and split a couple of them to make forked points, as he had done with the spear. He had no feathers so he just left them bare, figuring for fish they only had to travel a few inches. He had no string and that threw him until he looked down at his tennis shoes. They had long laces, too long, and he found that one lace cut in half would take care of both shoes and that left the other lace for a bowstring.

All seemed to be going well until he tried a test shot. He put an arrow to the string, pulled it back to his cheek, pointed it at a dirt hummock, and at that precise instant the bow wood exploded in his hands sending splinters and chips of wood into his face. Two pieces actually stuck into his forehead, just above his eyes, and had they been only slightly lower they would have blinded him.

◀ What mistake did Brian make with his first bow?

Too stiff.

Mistakes. In his mental journal he listed them to tell his father, listed all the mistakes. He had made a new bow, with slender limbs and a more fluid, gentle pull, but could not hit the fish though he sat in the water and was, in the end, surrounded by a virtual cloud of small fish. It was infuriating. He would pull the bow back, set the arrow just above the water, and when the fish was no more than an inch away release the arrow.

Only to miss. It seemed to him that the arrow had gone right through the fish, again and again, but the fish didn't get hurt. Finally, after hours, he stuck the arrow down in the water, pulled the bow, and waited for a fish to come close and while he was waiting he noticed that the water seemed to make the arrow bend or break in the middle.

Of course—he had forgotten that water refracts, bends light. He had learned that somewhere, in some

◀ What observation helped Brian aim correctly to kill the fish?

class, maybe it was biology—he couldn't remember. But it did bend light and that meant the fish were not where they appeared to be. They were lower, just below, which meant he had to aim just under them.

He would not forget his first hit. Not ever. A round-shaped fish, with golden sides, sides as gold as the sun, stopped in front of the arrow and he aimed just beneath it, at the bottom edge of the fish, and released the arrow and there was a bright flurry, a splash of gold in the water. He grabbed the arrow and raised it up and the fish was on the end, wiggling against the blue sky.

He held the fish against the sky until it stopped wiggling, held it and looked to the sky and felt his throat tighten, swell, and fill with pride at what he had done.

He had done food.

With his bow, with an arrow fashioned by his own hands he had done food, had found a way to live. The bow had given him this way and he <u>exulted</u> in it, in the bow, in the arrow, in the fish, in the hatchet, in the sky. He stood and walked from the water, still holding the fish and arrow and bow against the sky, seeing them as they fit his arms, as they were part of him.

He had food.

He cut a green willow fork and held the fish over the fire until the skin crackled and peeled away and the meat inside was flaky and moist and tender. This he picked off carefully with his fingers, tasting every piece, mashing them in his mouth with his tongue to get the juices out of them, hot steaming pieces of fish. . . .

He could not, he thought then, ever get enough. And all that first day, first new day, he spent going to the lake, shooting a fish, taking it back to the fire, cooking it and eating it, then back to the lake, shoot-

words for everyday use

ex • ult (ig zult') v., rejoice. The lottery winner <u>exulted</u> in his newfound wealth.

ing a fish, cooking it and eating it, and on that way until it was dark.

He had taken the scraps back to the water with the thought they might work for bait, and the other fish came by the hundreds to clean them up. He could take his pick of them. Like a store, he thought, just like a store, and he could not remember later how many he ate that day but he thought it must have been over twenty.

It had been a feast day, his first feast day, and a celebration of being alive and the new way he had of getting food. By the end of that day, when it became dark and he lay next to the fire with his stomach full of fish and grease from the meat smeared around his mouth, he could feel new hope building in him. Not hope that he would be rescued—that was gone.

But hope in his knowledge. Hope in the fact that he could learn and survive and take care of himself.

Tough hope, he thought that night. I am full of tough hope.

◀ *What did Brian celebrate? What new hope did he have?*

Chapter 14

Mistakes.

Small mistakes could turn into disasters, funny little mistakes could snowball so that while you were still smiling at the humor you could find yourself looking at death. In the city if he made a mistake usually there was a way to rectify it, make it all right. If he fell on his bike and sprained a leg he could wait for it to heal; if he forgot something at the store he could find other food in the refrigerator.

Now it was different, and all so quick, all so incredibly quick. If he sprained a leg here he might starve before he could get around again; if he missed while he was hunting or if the fish moved away he might starve. If he got sick, really sick so he couldn't move he might starve.

Mistakes.

Early in the new time he had learned the most important thing, the truly vital knowledge that drives all creatures in the forest—food is all. Food was simply everything. All things in the woods, from insects to fish to bears, were always, always looking for food—it was the great, single driving influence in nature. To eat. All must eat.

But the way he learned it almost killed him. His second new night, stomach full of fish and the fire smoldering in the shelter, he had been sound asleep when something—he thought later it might be smell—had awakened him.

▶ Why do mistakes matter more in the wilderness?

▶ What drives every creature in the forest?

Near the fire, completely unafraid of the smoking coals, completely unafraid of Brian, a skunk was digging where he had buried the eggs. There was some sliver of a moon and in the faint-pearl light he could see the bushy tail, the white stripes down the back, and he had nearly smiled. He did not know how the skunk had found the eggs, some smell, perhaps some tiny fragment of shell had left a smell, but it looked almost cute, its little head down and its little tail up as it dug and dug, kicking the sand back.

But those were his eggs, not the skunk's, and the half smile had been quickly replaced with fear that he would lose his food and he had grabbed a handful of sand and thrown it at the skunk.

"Get out of here . . ."

He was going to say more, some silly human words, but in less than half a second the skunk had snapped its rear end up, curved the tail over, and sprayed Brian with a direct shot aimed at his head from less than four feet away.

In the tiny confines of the shelter the effect was devastating. The thick sulfurous rotten odor filled the small room, heavy, ugly, and stinking. The <u>corrosive</u> spray that hit his face <u>seared</u> into his lungs and eyes, blinding him.

He screamed and threw himself sideways, taking the entire wall off the shelter; screamed and clawed out of the shelter and fell-ran to the shore of the lake. Stumbling and tripping, he scrambled into the water and slammed his head back and forth trying to wash his eyes, slashing at the water to clear his eyes.

A hundred funny cartoons he had seen about skunks. Cute cartoons about the smell of skunks, cartoons to laugh at and joke about, but when the spray hit there was nothing funny about it—he was completely blind for almost two hours. A lifetime. He thought that he might be permanently blind, or at least impaired—and that would have been the end.

◀ What made Brian smile? Why did he quickly change his attitude?

◀ What ideas had Brian had about skunks? What has he learned?

words for everyday use

cor • ro • sive (kə rō′ siv) *adj.,* having the power to eat away. *The <u>corrosive</u> chemicals quickly made a hole in the plastic.*

sear (si[ə]r) *v.,* burn or scorch. *The heat from the grill quickly <u>seared</u> the outside of the meat.*

As it was the pain in his eyes lasted for days, bothered him after that for two weeks. The smell in the shelter, in his clothes, and in his hair was still there now, almost a month and a half later.

And he had nearly smiled.

Mistakes.

Food had to be protected. While he was in the lake trying to clear his eyes the skunk went ahead and dug up the rest of the turtle eggs and ate every one. Licked all the shells clean and couldn't have cared less that Brian was thrashing around in the water like a dying carp. The skunk had found food and was taking it and Brian was paying for a lesson.

▶ What two things does Brian learn are important?

Protect food and have a good shelter. Not just a shelter to keep the wind and rain out, but a shelter to protect, a shelter to make him safe. The day after the skunk he set about making a good place to live.

The basic idea had been good, the place for his shelter was right, but he just hadn't gone far enough. He'd been lazy—but now he knew the second most important thing about nature, what drives nature. Food was first, but the work for the food went on and on. Nothing in nature was lazy. He had tried to take a shortcut and paid for it with his turtle eggs—which he had come to like more than chicken eggs from the store. They had been fuller somehow, had more depth to them.

▶ How does Brian learn a lesson about being lazy?

He set about improving his shelter by tearing it down. From dead pines up the hill he brought down heavier logs and fastened several of them across the opening, wedging them at the top and burying the bottoms in the sand. Then he wove long branches in through them to make a truly tight wall and, still not satisfied, he took even thinner branches and wove those into the first weave. When he was at last finished he could not find a place to put his fist through. It all held together like a very stiff woven basket.

He judged the door opening to be the weakest spot, and here he took special time to weave a door of willows in so tight a mesh that no matter how a skunk tried—or porcupine, he thought, looking at the marks in his leg—it could not possibly get through. He had no hinges but by arranging some cut-off limbs at the top in the right way he had a method to hook the door in place, and when he was in and the door was hung he felt relatively safe. A bear, something big, could still get in by tearing at it, but nothing small could bother him and the weave of the structure still allowed the smoke to filter up through the top and out.

All in all it took him three days to make the shelter, stopping to shoot fish and eat as he went, bathing four times a day to try to get the smell from the skunk to leave. When his house was done, finally done right, he turned to the constant problem—food.

It was all right to hunt and eat, or fish and eat, but what happened if he had to go a long time without food? What happened when the berries were gone and he got sick or hurt or—thinking of the skunk—laid up temporarily? He needed a way to store food, a place to store it, and he needed food to store.

◄ Why does Brian need to store food?

Mistakes.

He tried to learn from the mistakes. He couldn't bury food again, couldn't leave it in the shelter, because something like a bear could get at it right away. It had to be high, somehow, high and safe.

Above the door to the shelter, up the rock face about ten feet, was a small ledge that could make a natural storage place, unreachable to animals—except that it was unreachable to him as well.

A ladder, of course. He needed a ladder. But he had no way to fashion one, nothing to hold the steps on, and that stopped him until he found a dead pine with many small branches still sticking out. Using his hatchet he chopped the branches off so they stuck out four or five inches, all up along the log, then he cut the log off about ten feet long and dragged it down to his shelter. It was a little heavy, but dry and he could manage it, and when he propped it up he found he could climb to the ledge with ease, though the tree did roll from side to side a bit as he climbed.

His food shelf—as he thought of it—had been covered with bird manure and he carefully scraped it clean with sticks. He had never seen birds there, but

▶ *Of what is Brian proud?*

that was probably because the smoke from his fire went up right across the opening and they didn't like smoke. Still, he had learned and he took time to weave a snug door for the small opening with green willows, cutting it so it jammed in tightly, and when he finished he stood back and looked at the rock face—his shelter below, the food shelf above—and allowed a small bit of pride to come.

Not bad, he had thought, not bad for somebody who used to have trouble greasing the bearings on his bicycle. Not bad at all.

Mistakes.

He had made a good shelter and food shelf, but he had no food except for fish and the last of the berries. And the fish, as good as they still tasted then, were not something he could store. His mother had left some salmon out by mistake one time when they went on an overnight trip to Cape Hesper to visit relatives and when they got back the smell filled the whole house. There was no way to store fish.

At least, he thought, no way to store them dead. But as he looked at the weave of his structure a thought came to him and he moved down to the water.

He had been putting the waste from the fish back in the water and the food had attracted hundreds of new ones.

"I wonder . . ."

They seemed to come easily to the food, at least the small ones. He had no trouble now shooting them and had even speared one with his old fish spear now that he knew to aim low. He could dangle something in his fingers and they came right up to it. It might be possible, he thought, might just be possible to trap them. Make some kind of pond . . .

To his right, at the base of the rock bluff, there were piles of smaller rocks that had fallen from the main chunk, splinters and hunks, from double-fist size to some as large as his head. He spent an afternoon carrying rocks to the beach and making what amounted to a large pen for holding live fish—two rock "arms" that stuck out fifteen feet into the lake and curved together at the end. Where the arms came together he left an opening about two feet across, then he sat on the shore and waited.

When he had first started dropping the rocks all the fish had darted away. But his fish-trash pile of bones and skin and guts was in the pond area and the prospect of food brought them back. Soon, under an hour, there were thirty or forty small fish in the enclosure and Brian made a gate by weaving small willows together into a fine mesh and closed them in.

"Fresh fish," he had yelled. "I have fresh fish for sale . . ."

Storing live fish to eat later had been a major breakthrough, he thought. It wasn't just keeping from starving—it was trying to save ahead, think ahead.

Of course he didn't know then how sick he would get of fish.

◄ *Why is making the fish pond a breakthrough?*

---

words for everyday use   pros • pect (präs' pekt) *n.*, anticipation; possibility. *The prospect of a hot meal and a dry bed motivated us to move quickly on the way home.*

Chapter 15

The days had folded one into another and mixed so that after two or three weeks he only knew time had passed in days because he made a mark for each day in the stone near the door to his shelter. Real time he measured in events. A day was nothing, not a thing to remember—it was just sun coming up, sun going down, some light in the middle.

▶ How does Brian measure time?

But events—events were burned into his memory and so he used them to remember time, to know and to remember what had happened, to keep a mental journal.

There had been the day of First Meat. That had been a day that had started like the rest, up after the sun, clean the camp and make sure there is enough wood for another night. But it was a long time, a long time of eating fish and looking for berries, and he craved more, craved more food, heavier food, deeper food.

He craved meat. He thought in the night now of meat, thought of his mother's cooking a roast or dreamed of turkey, and one night he awakened before he had to put wood on the fire with his mouth making saliva and the taste of pork chops in his mouth. So real, so real. And all a dream, but it left him intent on getting meat.

▶ What does Brian's dream inspire him to do?

He had been working farther and farther out for wood, sometimes now going nearly a quarter of a mile away from camp for wood, and he saw many small animals. Squirrels were everywhere, small red ones that chattered at him and seemed to swear and jumped from limb to limb. There were also many rabbits—large, gray ones with a mix of reddish fur, smaller fast gray ones that he saw only at dawn. The larger ones sometimes sat until he was quite close, then bounded and jerked two or three steps before freezing again. He thought if he worked at it and practiced he might hit one of the larger rabbits with an arrow or a spear—never the small ones or the squirrels. They were too small and fast.

Then there were the foolbirds.

They exasperated him to the point where they were close to driving him insane. The birds were everywhere, five and six in a flock, and their camouflage was so perfect that it was possible for Brian to sit and rest, leaning against a tree, with one of them standing right in front of him in a willow clump, two feet away—hidden—only to explode into deafening flight just when Brian least expected it. He just couldn't see them, couldn't figure out how to locate them before they flew, because they stood so perfectly still and blended in so perfectly well.

◄ Why are the "foolbirds" so frustrating?

And what made it worse was that they were so dumb, or seemed to be so dumb, that it was almost insulting the way they kept hidden from him. Nor could he get used to the way they exploded up when they flew. It seemed like every time he went for wood, which was every morning, he spent the whole time jumping and jerking in fright as he walked. On one memorable morning he had actually reached for a piece of wood, what he thought to be a pitchy stump at the base of a dead birch, his fingers close to touching it, only to have it blow up in his face.

But on the day of First Meat he had decided the best thing to try for would be a foolbird and that morning he had set out with his bow and spear to get one; to stay with it until he got one and ate some meat. Not to get wood, not to find berries, but to get a bird and eat some meat.

At first the hunt had not gone well. He saw plenty of birds, working up along the shore of the lake to the end, then down the other side, but he only saw

◄ Why didn't the hunt go well?

them after they flew. He had to find a way to see them first, see them and get close enough to either shoot them with the bow or use the spear, and he could not find a way to see them.

When he had gone halfway around the lake, and had jumped up twenty or so birds, he finally gave up and sat at the base of a tree. He had to work this out, see what he was doing wrong. There were birds there, and he had eyes—he just had to bring the two things together.

Looking wrong, he thought. I am looking wrong. More, more than that I am being wrong somehow— I am doing it the wrong way. Fine—sarcasm came into his thoughts—I know that, thank you. I know I'm doing it wrong. But what is right? The morning sun had cooked him until it seemed his brain was frying, sitting by the tree, but nothing came until he got up and started to walk again and hadn't gone two steps when a bird got up. It had been there all the time, while he was thinking about how to see them, right next to him—right there.

He almost screamed.

▶ What was the key to hunting the foolbirds?

But this time, when the bird flew, something caught his eye and it was the secret key. The bird cut down toward the lake, then, seeing it couldn't land in the water, turned and flew back up the hill into the trees. When it turned, curving through the trees, the sun had caught it, and Brian, for an instant, saw it as a shape; sharp-pointed in front, back from the head in a streamlined bullet shape to the fat body.

Kind of like a pear, he had thought, with a point on one end and a fat little body; a flying pear.

And that had been the secret. He had been looking for feathers, for the color of the bird, for a bird sitting there. He had to look for the outline instead, had to see the shape instead of the feathers or color, had to train his eyes to see the shape . . .

It was like turning on a television. Suddenly, he could see things he never saw before. In just moments, it seemed, he saw three birds before they flew, saw them sitting and got close to one of them, moving slowly, got close enough to try a shot with his bow.

He had missed that time, and had missed many more, but he saw them; he saw the little fat shapes with the pointed heads sitting in the brush all over the place. Time and again he drew, held, and let arrows fly but he still had no feathers on the arrows and they were little more than sticks that flopped out of the bow, sometimes going sideways. Even when a bird was seven or eight feet away the arrow would turn without feathers to stabilize it and hit brush or a twig. After a time he gave up with the bow. It had worked all right for the fish, when they came right to the end of the arrow, but it wasn't good for any kind of distance—at least not the way it was now.

But he had carried his fish spear, the original one with the two prongs, and he moved the bow to his left hand and carried the spear in his right.

He tried throwing the spear but he was not good enough and not fast enough—the birds could fly amazingly fast, get up fast. But in the end he found that if he saw the bird sitting and moved sideways toward it—not directly toward it but at an angle, back and forth—he could get close enough to put the spear point out ahead almost to the bird and thrust-lunge with it. He came close twice, and then, down along the lake not far from the beaver house he got his first meat.

◀ How did Brian kill the bird?

The bird had sat and he had lunged and the two points took the bird back down into the ground and killed it almost instantly—it had fluttered a bit—and Brian had grabbed it and held it in both hands until he was sure it was dead.

Then he picked up the spear and the bow and trotted back around the lake to his shelter, where the fire had burned down to glowing coals. He sat looking at the bird wondering what to do. With the fish, he had just cooked them whole, left everything in and picked the meat off. This was different; he would have to clean it.

It had always been so simple at home. He would go to the store and get a chicken and it was all cleaned and neat, no feathers or insides, and his mother would bake it in the oven and he would eat it. His mother from the old time, from the time before, would bake it.

Now he had the bird, but he had never cleaned one, never taken the insides out or gotten rid of the feathers, and he didn't know where to start. But he wanted the meat—had to have the meat—and that drove him.

In the end the feathers came off easily. He tried to pluck them out but the skin was so fragile that it pulled off as well, so he just pulled the skin off the bird. Like peeling an orange, he thought, sort of. Except that when the skin was gone the insides fell out the back end.

He was immediately caught in a cloud of raw odor, a kind of steamy dung odor that came up from the greasy coil of insides that fell from the bird, and he nearly threw up. But there was something else to the smell as well, some kind of richness that went with his hunger and that overcame the sick smell.

He quickly cut the neck with his hatchet, cut the feet off the same way, and in his hand he held something like a small chicken with a dark, fat, thick breast and small legs.

He set it up on some sticks on the shelter wall and took the feathers and insides down to the water, to his fish pond. The fish would eat them, or eat what they could, and the feeding action would bring more fish. On second thought he took out the wing and tail feathers, which were stiff and long and pretty—banded and speckled in browns and grays and light reds. There might be some use for them, he thought, maybe work them onto the arrows somehow.

The rest he threw in the water, saw the small round fish begin tearing at it, and washed his hands. Back at the shelter the flies were on the meat and he brushed them off. It was amazing how fast they came, but when he built up the fire and the smoke increased the flies almost magically disappeared. He pushed a pointed stick through the bird and held it over the fire.

The fire was too hot. The flames hit the fat and the bird almost ignited. He held it higher but the heat was worse and finally he moved it to the side a bit

▶ What drove Brian to figure out how to clean the bird?

▶ Why did Brian save the feathers?

and there it seemed to cook properly. Except that it only cooked on one side and all the juice dripped off. He had to rotate it slowly and that was hard to do with his hands so he found a forked stick and stuck it in the sand to put his cooking stick in. He turned it, and in this way he found a proper method to cook the bird.

In minutes the outside was cooked and the odor that came up was almost the same as the odor when his mother baked chickens in the oven and he didn't think he could stand it but when he tried to pull a piece of the breast meat off the meat was still raw inside.

Patience, he thought. So much of this was patience—waiting and thinking and doing things right. So much of all this, so much of all living was patience and thinking.

◀ What is much of life about?

He settled back, turning the bird slowly, letting the juices go back into the meat, letting it cook and smell and smell and cook and there came a time when it didn't matter if the meat was done or not; it was black on the outside and hard and hot, and he would eat it.

He tore a piece from the breast, a sliver of meat, and put it in his mouth and chewed carefully, chewed as slowly and carefully as he could to get all the taste and he thought:

Never. Never in all the food, all the hamburgers and malts, all the fries or meals at home, never in all the candy or pies or cakes, never in all the roasts or steaks or pizzas, never in all the submarine sandwiches, never never never had he tasted anything as fine as that first bite.

◀ How did the bird taste to Brian?

First Meat.

Chapter 16

And now he stood at the end of the long part of the lake and was not the same, would not be the same again.

There had been many First Days.

First Arrow Day—when he had used thread from his tattered old piece of windbreaker and some pitch from a stump to put slivers of feathers on a dry willow shaft and make an arrow that would fly correctly. Not accurately—he never got really good with it— but fly correctly so that if a rabbit or a foolbird sat in one place long enough, close enough, and he had enough arrows, he could hit it.

That brought First Rabbit Day—when he killed one of the large rabbits with an arrow and skinned it as he had the first bird, cooked it the same to find the meat as good—not as rich as the bird, but still good— and there were strips of fat on the back of the rabbit that cooked into the meat to make it richer.

Now he went back and forth between rabbits and foolbirds when he could, filling in with fish in the middle.

Always hungry.

I am always hungry but I can do it now, I can get food and I know I can get food and it makes me more. I know what I can do.

He moved closer to the lake to a stand of nut brush. These were thick bushes with little stickler pods that held green nuts—nuts that he thought he

▶ What are some "First Days" that Brian has had?

▶ How does Brian feel about his chances of survival?

might be able to eat but they weren't ripe yet. He was out for a foolbird and they liked to hide in the base of the thick part of the nut brush, back in where the stems were close together and provided cover.

In the second clump he saw a bird, moved close to it, paused when the head feathers came up and it made a sound like a cricket—a sign of alarm just before it flew—then moved closer when the feathers went down and the bird relaxed. He did this four times, never looking at the bird directly, moving toward it at an angle so that it seemed he was moving off to the side—he had perfected this method after many attempts and it worked so well that he had actually caught one with his bare hands—until he was standing less than three feet from the bird, which was frozen in a hiding attitude in the brush.

The bird held for him and he put an arrow to the bow, one of the feathered arrows, not a fish arrow, and drew and released. It was a clean miss and he took another arrow out of the cloth pouch, at his belt, which he'd made from a piece of his windbreaker sleeve, tied at one end to make a bottom. The foolbird sat still for him and he did not look directly at it until he drew the second arrow and aimed and released and missed again.

This time the bird jerked a bit and the arrow stuck next to it so close it almost brushed its breast. Brian only had two more arrows and he debated moving slowly to change the spear over to his right hand and use that to kill the bird. One more shot, he decided, he would try it again. He slowly brought another arrow out, put it on the string, and aimed and released and this time saw the flurry of feathers that meant he had made a hit.

The bird had been struck off-center and was flopping around wildly. Brian jumped on it and grabbed it and slammed it against the ground once, sharply, to kill it. Then he stood and retrieved his arrows and made sure they were all right and went down to the lake to wash the blood off his hands. He kneeled at the water's edge and put the dead bird and his weapons down and dipped his hands into the water.

▶ What was nearly
the last act of
Brian's life?

It was very nearly the last act of his life. Later he would not know why he started to turn—some smell or sound. A tiny brushing sound. But something caught his ear or nose and he began to turn, and had his head half around, when he saw a brown wall of fur detach itself from the forest to his rear and come down on him like a runaway truck. He just had time to see that it was a moose—he knew them from pictures but did not know, could not guess how large they were—when it hit him. It was a cow and she had no horns, but she took him in the left side of the back with her forehead, took him and threw him out into the water and then came after him to finish the job.

▶ What does the
moose do to Brian?

He had another half-second to fill his lungs with air and she was on him again, using her head to drive him down into the mud of the bottom. Insane, he thought. Just that, the word, insane. Mud filled his eyes, his ears, the horn boss on the moose drove him deeper and deeper into the bottom muck, and suddenly it was over and he felt alone.

He sputtered to the surface, sucking air and fighting panic, and when he wiped the mud and water out of his eyes and cleared them he saw the cow standing sideways to him, not ten feet away, calmly chewing on a lilypad root. She didn't appear to even see him, or didn't seem to care about him, and Brian turned carefully and began to swim-crawl out of the water.

As soon as he moved, the hair on her back went up and she charged him again, using her head and front hooves this time, slamming him back and down into the water, on his back this time, and he screamed the air out of his lungs and hammered on her head with his fists and filled his throat with water and she left again.

Once more he came to the surface. But he was hurt now, hurt inside, hurt in his ribs and he stayed hunched over, pretended to be dead. She was standing again, eating. Brian studied her out of one eye, looking to the bank with the other, wondering how seriously he was injured, wondering if she would let him go this time.

Insane.

He started to move, ever so slowly; her head turned and her back hair went up—like the hair on an angry dog—and he stopped, took a slow breath, the hair went down and she ate. Move, hair up, stop, hair down, move, hair up—a half-foot at a time until he was at the edge of the water. He stayed on his hands and knees—indeed, was hurt so he wasn't sure he could walk anyway, and she seemed to accept that and let him crawl, slowly, out of the water and up into the trees and brush.

◀ What word does Brian use to describe the moose's actions?

When he was behind a tree he stood carefully and took stock. Legs seemed all right, but his ribs were hurt bad—he could only take short breaths and then he had a jabbing pain—and his right shoulder seemed to be wrenched somehow. Also his bow and spear and foolbird were in the water.

◀ What injuries does Brian have after the moose attack?

At least he could walk and he had just about decided to leave everything when the cow moved out of the deeper water and left him, as quickly as she'd come, walking down along the shoreline in the shallow water, with her long legs making sucking sounds when she pulled them free of the mud. Hanging on a pine limb, he watched her go, half expecting her to turn and come back to run over him again. But she kept going and when she was well gone from sight he went to the bank and found the bird, then waded out a bit to get his bow and spear. Neither of them were broken and the arrows, incredibly, were still on his belt in the pouch, although messed up with mud and water.

It took him most of an hour to work his way back around the lake. His legs worked well enough, but if he took two or three fast steps he would begin to breath deeply and the pain from his ribs would stop him and he would have to lean against a tree until he could slow back down to shallow breathing. She had done more damage than he had originally thought, the insane cow—no sense at all to it. Just madness. When he got to the shelter he crawled inside and was grateful that the coals were still glowing and that he had thought to get wood first thing in the mornings

▶ For what is Brian grateful?

to be ready for the day, grateful that he had thought to get enough wood for two or three days at a time, grateful that he had fish nearby if he needed to eat, grateful, finally, as he dozed off, that he was alive.

So insane, he thought, letting sleep cover the pain in his chest—such an insane attack for no reason and he fell asleep with his mind trying to make the moose have reason.

▶ What noise does Brian hear? What does he feel he should do?

The noise awakened him.

It was a low sound, a low roaring sound that came from wind. His eyes snapped open not because it was loud but because it was new. He had felt wind in his shelter, felt the rain that came with wind and had heard thunder many times in the past forty-seven days but not this, not this noise. Low, almost alive, almost from a throat somehow, the sound, the noise was a roar, a far-off roar but coming at him and when he was fully awake he sat up in the darkness, <u>grimacing</u> with pain from his ribs.

The pain was different now, a tightened pain, and it seemed less—but the sound. So strange, he thought. A mystery sound. A spirit sound. A bad sound. He took some small wood and got the fire going again, felt some little comfort and cheer from the flames but also felt that he should get ready. He did not know how, but he should get ready. The sound was coming for him, was coming just for him, and he had to get ready. The sound wanted him.

He found the spear and bow where they were hanging on the pegs of the shelter wall and brought his weapons to the bed he had made of pine boughs. More comfort, but like the comfort of the flames it didn't work with this new threat that he didn't understand yet.

Restless threat, he thought, and stood out of the shelter away from the flames to study the sky but it was too dark. The sound meant something to

---

words for everyday use **gri • mace** (grim′ əs) v., to make a facial expression of disgust, disapproval, or pain. *Fiona <u>grimaced</u> at Thor's terrible idea.*

him, something from his memory, something he had read about. Something he had seen on television. Something . . . oh, he thought. Oh no.

It was wind, wind like the sound of a train, with the low belly roar of a train. It was a tornado. That was it! The roar of a train meant bad wind and it was coming for him. God, he thought, on top of the moose not this—not this.

◀ What does Brian realize he is hearing?

But it was too late, too late to do anything. In the strange stillness he looked to the night sky, then turned back into his shelter and was leaning over to go through the door opening when it hit. Later he would think of it and find that it was the same as the moose. Just insanity. He was taken in the back by some mad force and driven into the shelter on his face, slammed down into the pine branches of his bed.

◀ How is the tornado like the moose?

At the same time the wind tore at the fire and sprayed red coals and sparks in a cloud around him. Then it backed out, seemed to hesitate momentarily, and returned with a massive roar; a roar that took his ears and mind and body.

He was whipped against the front wall of the shelter like a rag, felt a ripping pain in his ribs again, then was hammered back down into the sand once more while the wind took the whole wall, his bed, the fire, his tools—all of it—and threw it out into the lake, gone out of sight, gone forever. He felt a burning on his neck and reached up to find red coals there. He brushed those off, found more in his pants, brushed those away, and the wind hit again, heavy gusts, tearing gusts. He heard trees snapping in the forest around the rock, felt his body slipping out and clawed at the rocks to hold himself down. He couldn't think, just held and knew that he was praying but didn't know what the prayer was—knew that he wanted to be, stay and be, and then the wind moved to the lake.

Brian heard the great, roaring sucking sounds of water and opened his eyes to see the lake torn by the wind, the water slamming in great waves that went in all ways, fought each other and then rose in a spout of water going up into the night sky like a wet column of light. It was beautiful and terrible at the same time.

The tornado tore one more time at the shore on the opposite side of the lake—Brian could hear trees being ripped down—and then it was done, gone as rapidly as it had come. It left nothing, nothing but Brian in the pitch dark. He could find nothing of where his fire had been, not a spark, nothing of his shelter, tools, or bed, even the body of the foolbird was gone. I am back to nothing he thought, trying to find things in the dark—back to where I was when I crashed. Hurt, in the dark, just the same.

As if to emphasize his thoughts the mosquitos—with the fire gone and protective smoke no longer saving him—came back in thick, nostril-clogging swarms. All that was left was the hatchet at his belt. Still there. But now it began to rain and in the downpour he would never find anything dry enough to get a fire going, and at last he pulled his battered body back in under the overhang, where his bed had been, and wrapped his arms around his ribs.

Sleep didn't come, couldn't come with the insects ripping at him, so he lay the rest of the night, slapping mosquitos and chewing with his mind on the day. This morning he had been fat—well, almost fat—and happy, sure of everything, with good weapons and food and the sun in his face and things looking good for the future, and inside of one day, just one day, he had been run over by a moose and a tornado, had lost everything and was back to square one. Just like that.

A flip of some giant coin and he was the loser.

But there is a difference now, he thought—there really is a difference. I might be hit but I'm not done. When the light comes I'll start to rebuild. I still have the hatchet and that's all I had in the first place.

Come on, he thought, baring his teeth in the darkness—come on. Is that the best you can do? Is that all you can hit me with—a moose and a tornado? Well, he thought, holding his ribs and smiling, then spitting mosquitos out of his mouth. Well, that won't get the job done. That was the difference now. He had changed, and he was tough. I'm tough where it counts—tough in the head.

▶ Describe Brian's situation after the tornado comes through.

▶ How has Brian's situation changed in one day?

▶ Why is Brian in better shape than when the plane first crashed?

In the end, right before dawn a kind of cold snap came down—something else new, this cold snap—and the mosquitos settled back into the damp grass and under the leaves and he could sleep. Or doze. And the last thought he had that morning as he closed his eyes was: I hope the tornado hit the moose.

When he awakened the sun was cooking the inside of his mouth and had dried his tongue to leather. He had fallen into a deeper sleep with his mouth open just at dawn and it tasted as if he had been sucking on his foot all night.

He rolled out and almost bellowed with pain from his ribs. They had tightened in the night and seemed to pull at his chest when he moved. He slowed his movements and stood slowly, without stretching unduly, and went to the lake for a drink. At the shore he kneeled, carefully and with great gentleness, and drank and rinsed his mouth. To his right he saw that the fish pond was still there, although the willow gate was gone and there were no fish. They'll come back, he thought, as soon as I can make a spear or bow and get one or two for bait they'll come back.

He turned to look at his shelter—saw that some of the wood for the wall was scattered around the beach but was still there, then saw his bow jammed into a driftwood log, broken but with the precious string still intact. Not so bad now—not so bad. He looked down the shoreline for other parts of his wall and that's when he saw it.

Out in the lake, in the short part of the L, something curved and yellow was sticking six or eight inches out of the water. It was a bright color, not an earth or natural color, and for a second he could not place it, then he knew it for what it was.

◀ *What does Brian notice in the lake?*

"It's the tail of the plane." He said it aloud, half expecting to hear somebody answer him. There it was, sticking up out of the water. The tornado must have flipped the plane around somehow when it hit the lake, changed the position of the plane and raised the tail. Well, he thought. Well, just look at that. And at the same moment a cutting thought hit him. He thought of the pilot, still in the plane, and that brought a shiver and massive sadness that seemed to settle on him like a weight and he thought that he should say or do something for the pilot; some words but he didn't know any of the right words, the religious words.

So he went down to the side of the water and looked at the plane and focused his mind, the way he did when he was hunting the foolbirds and wanted to concentrate, focused it on the pilot and thought: Have rest. Have rest forever.

▶ *What words does Brian say for the pilot?*

Respond to the Selection

If you were writing a biography of Brian, with a chapter describing his experiences in the wilderness, what would you call that chapter? Why?

Investigate, Inquire, and Imagine

Recall: GATHER FACTS

1a. What drives every creature in the forest?

2a. What are some of the mistakes Brian has made?

3a. What does Brian see in the lake after the tornado?

Interpret: FIND MEANING

1b. How did Brian learn what drives every forest creature? Why does it matter to him?

2b. Why do mistakes matter more in the forest?

3b. How might this affect Brian?

Analyze: TAKE THINGS APART

4a. List some of the "First Days" Brian has.

Synthesize: BRING THINGS TOGETHER

4b. Why are Brian's "First Days" important to him?

Evaluate: MAKE JUDGMENTS

5a. Is Brian's situation after the tornado better than his situation after the crash? In a chart like the one below, list ways in which the two situations are similar and different.

Extend: CONNECT IDEAS

5b. What would the "old Brian" have done after the tornado?

Similarities	Differences

Understanding Literature

DESCRIPTION. **Description** is a type of writing that portrays a character, object, or scene. Descriptions make use of *sensory details*—words and phrases that describe how things look, sound, smell, taste, or feel. Reread pages 101–105. What do the foolbirds look like? What do they act like? What vivid words and phrases does Paulsen use as he describes how Brian skins, prepares, cooks, and eats the bird?

Chapter 17

He turned back to his campsite and looked to the wreckage. He had a lot to do, rebuild his shelter, get a new fire going, find some food or get ready to find some food, make weapons—and he had to work slowly because his ribs hurt.

First things first. He tried to find some dry grass and twigs, then peeled bark from a nearby birch to shred into a fire nest. He worked slowly but even so, with his new skill he had a fire going in less than an hour. The flames cut the cool damp morning, crackled and did much to bring his spirits up, not to mention chasing away the <u>incessant</u> mosquitos. With the fire going he searched for dry wood—the rain had driven water into virtually all the wood he could find—and at last located some in a thick evergreen where the top branches had covered the lower dead ones, keeping them dry.

He had great difficulty breaking them, not being able to pull much with his arm or chest muscles, but finally got enough to keep the fire going all day and into the night. With that he rested a bit, eased his chest, and then set about getting a shelter squared away.

◄ What does Brian have to do the day after the tornado?

words for everyday use
in • ces • sant (in ses' ənt) *adj.*, continuing without interruption. *The sound of the sea moving up and down the shore is* <u>incessant</u>.

▶ Why does Brian feel lucky?

Much of the wood from his original wall was still nearby and up in back of the ridge he actually found a major section of the weave still intact. The wind had torn it out, lifted it, and thrown it to the top of the ridge and Brian felt lucky once more that he had not been killed or more seriously injured—which would have been the same, he thought. If he couldn't hunt he would die and if he were injured badly he would not be able to hunt.

He jerked and dragged wood around until the wall was once more in place—crudely, but he could improve it later. He had no trouble finding enough pine boughs to make a new bed. The storm had torn the forest to pieces—up in back of the ridge it looked like a giant had become angry and used some kind of a massive meatgrinder on the trees. Huge pines were twisted and snapped off, blown sideways. The ground was so littered, with limbs and tree-tops sticking every which way, that it was hard to get through. He pulled enough thick limbs in for a bed, green and spicy with the new broken sap smell, and by evening he was exhausted, hungry, and hurting, but he had something close to a place to live again, a place to be.

▶ What does the storm damage look like to Brian?

Tomorrow, he thought, as he lay back in the darkness. Tomorrow maybe the fish would be back and he would make a spear and new bow and get some food. Tomorrow he would find food and refine the camp and bring things back to sanity from the one completely insane day.

He faced the fire. Curving his body, he rested his head on his arm, and began to sleep when a picture came into his head. The tail of the plane sticking out of the water. There it was, the tail sticking up. And inside the plane, near the tail somewhere, was the survival pack. It must have survived the crash because the plane's main body was still intact. That was the picture—the tail sticking up and the survival pack inside—right there in his mind as he dozed. His eyes snapped open. If I could get at the pack, he thought. Oh, if I could get at the pack. It probably had food and knives and matches. It might have a sleeping bag. It might have fishing gear. Oh, it must

▶ What does Brian hope to get from the plane wreck?

have so many wonderful things—if I could get at the pack and just get some of those things. I would be rich. So rich if I could get at the pack.

Tomorrow. He watched the flames and smiled. Tomorrow I'll see. All things come tomorrow.

He slept, deep and down with only the picture of the plane tail sticking up in his mind. A healing sleep.

In the morning he rolled out before true light. In the gray dawn he built up the fire and found more wood for the day, feeling almost <u>chipper</u> because his ribs were much better now. With camp ready for the day he looked to the lake. Part of him half-expected the plane tail to be gone, sunk back into the depths, but he saw that it was still there, didn't seem to have moved at all.

He looked down at his feet and saw that there were some fish in his fish pen looking for the tiny bits of bait still left from before the wind came. He fought impatience to get on the plane project and remembered sense, remembered what he had learned. First food, because food made strength; first food, then thought, then action. There were fish at hand here, and he might not be able to get anything from the plane. That was all a dream.

The fish were real and his stomach, even his new shrunken stomach, was sending signals that it was savagely empty.

He made a fish spear with two points, not peeling the bark all the way back but just working on the pointed end. It took him an hour or so and all the time he worked he sat looking at the tail of the plane sticking up in the air, his hands working on the spear, his mind working on the problem of the plane.

When the spear was done, although still crude, he jammed a wedge between the points to spread them apart and went to the fish pond. There were not

◄ Why does Brian stop to get food before going to the plane?

words for everyday use

chip • per (chip' ər) adj., happy and lighthearted. It was surprising to see Lisa, a non-morning person, so <u>chipper</u> at dawn.

clouds of fish, but at least ten, and he picked one of the larger ones, a round fish almost six inches long, and put the spear point in the water, held it, then thrust with a flicking motion of his wrist when the fish was just above the point.

The fish was pinned neatly and he took two more with the same ease, then carried all three back up to the fire. He had a fish board now, a piece of wood he had flattened with the hatchet, that leaned up by the fire for cooking fish so he didn't have to hold a stick all the time. He put the three fish on the board, pushed sharpened pegs through their tails into cracks on the cooking board, and propped it next to the reddest part of the coals. In moments the fish were hissing and cooking with the heat and as soon as they were done, or when he could stand the smell no longer, he picked the steaming meat from under the loosened skin and ate it.

The fish did not fill him, did not even come close—fish meat was too light for that. But they gave him strength—he could feel it moving into his arms and legs—and he began to work on the plane project.

▶ What does Brian need to build in order to carry out his "plane project"?

While making the spear he had decided that what he would have to do was make a raft and push-paddle the raft to the plane and tie it there for a working base. Somehow he would have to get into the tail, inside the plane—rip or cut his way in—and however he did it he would need an operating base of some kind. A raft.

Which, he found ruefully, was much easier said than done. There were plenty of logs around. The shore was littered with driftwood, new and old, tossed up and scattered by the tornado. And it was a simple matter to find four of them about the same length and pull them together.

▶ What has Brian learned about solving problems?

Keeping them together was the problem. Without rope or crosspieces and nails the logs just rolled and separated. He tried wedging them together, crossing them over each other—nothing seemed to work. And he needed a stable platform to get the job done. It was becoming frustrating and he had a momentary loss of temper—as he would have done in the past, when he was the other person.

At that point he sat back on the beach and studied the problem again. Sense, he had to use his sense. That's all it took to solve problems—just sense.

It came then. The logs he had selected were smooth and round and had no limbs. What he needed were logs with limbs sticking out, then he could cross the limbs of one log over the limbs of another and "weave" them together as he had done his wall, the food shelf cover, and the fish gate. He scanned the area above the beach and found four dry treetops that had been broken off by the storm. These had limbs and he dragged them down to his work area at the water's edge and fitted them together.

It took most of the day. The limbs were cluttered and stuck any which way and he would have to cut one to make another fit, then cut one from another log to come back to the first one, then still another from a third log would have to be pulled in.

◀ What does Brian call the raft? Why?

But at last, in the late afternoon he was done and the raft—which he called Brushpile One for its looks—hung together even as he pulled it into the water off the beach. It floated well, if low in the water, and in the excitement he started for the plane. He could not stand on it, but would have to swim alongside.

He was out to chest depth when he realized he had no way to keep the raft at the plane. He needed some way to tie it in place so he could work from it.

And for a moment he was <u>stymied</u>. He had no rope, only the bowstring and the other cut shoestring in his tennis shoes—which were by now looking close to dead, his toes showing at the tops. Then he remembered his windbreaker and he found the tattered part he used for an arrow pouch. He tore it into narrow strips and tied them together to make a rope or tie-down about four feet long. It wasn't

---

words for everyday use   sty • mie (stī′ mē) v., to stand in the way of. *The sudden thunderstorm stymied Amy's plans for a picnic.*

strong, he couldn't use it to pull a Tarzan and swing from a tree, but it should hold the raft to the plane.

Once more he slid the raft off the beach and out into the water until he was chest deep. He had left his tennis shoes in the shelter and when he felt the sand turn to mud between his toes he kicked off the bottom and began to swim.

▶ *Why does Brian decide to wait to go to the plane?*

Pushing the raft, he figured, was about like trying to push an aircraft carrier. All the branches that stuck down into the water dragged and pulled and the logs themselves fought any forward motion and he hadn't gone twenty feet when he realized that it was going to be much harder than he thought to get the raft to the plane. It barely moved and if he kept going this way he would just about reach the plane at dark. He decided to turn back again, spend the night and start early in the morning, and he pulled the raft once more onto the sand and wipe-scraped it dry with his hand.

Patience. He was better now but impatience still ground at him a bit so he sat at the edge of the fish pond with the new spear and took three more fish, cooked them up and ate them, which helped to pass the time until dark. He also dragged in more wood—endless wood—and then relaxed and watched the sun set over the trees in back of the ridge. West, he thought. I'm watching the sun set in the west. And that way was north where his father was, and that way east and that way south—and somewhere to the south and east his mother would be. The news would be on the television. He could visualize more easily his mother doing things than his father because he had never been to where his father lived now. He knew everything about how his mother lived. She would have the small television on the kitchen counter on and be watching the news and talking about how awful it was in South Africa or how cute the baby in the commercial looked. Talking and making sounds, cooking sounds.

He jerked his mind back to the lake. There was great beauty here—almost unbelievable beauty. The sun exploded the sky, just blew it up with the setting color, and that color came down into the water of the lake, lit the trees. Amazing beauty and he wished he could share it with somebody and say, "Look there, and over there, and see that . . ."

But even alone it was beautiful and he fed the fire to cut the night chill. There it is again, he thought, that late summer chill to the air, the smell of fall. He went to sleep thinking a kind of reverse question. He did not know if he would ever get out of this, could not see how it might be, but if he did somehow get home and go back to living the way he had lived, would it be just the opposite? Would he be sitting watching television and suddenly think about the sunset up in back of the ridge and wonder how the color looked in the lake?

Sleep.

◀ What does Brian wonder about going back to his life?

In the morning the chill was more pronounced and he could see tiny wisps of vapor from his breath. He threw wood on the fire and blew until it flamed, then banked the flames to last and went down to the lake. Perhaps because the air was so cool the water felt warm as he waded in. He made sure the hatchet was still at his belt and the raft still held together, then set out pushing the raft and kick-swimming toward the tail of the plane.

As before, it was very hard going. Once an eddy[1] of breeze came up against him and he seemed to be standing still and by the time he was close enough to the tail to see the rivets in the aluminum he had pushed and kicked for over two hours, was nearly exhausted and wished he had taken some time to get a fish or two and have breakfast. He was also wrinkled as a prune and ready for a break.

The tail looked much larger when he got next to it, with a major part of the vertical stabilizer showing and perhaps half of the elevators. Only a short piece of the top of the fuselage, the plane's body toward the tail, was out of the water, just a curve of aluminum, and at first he could see no place to tie the raft. But he pulled himself along the elevators to the

---

1. **eddy.** A current of air or water running against the main current or in a circle

end and there he found a gap that went in up by the hinges where he could feed his rope through.

With the raft secure he climbed on top of it and lay on his back for fifteen minutes, resting and letting the sun warm him. The job, he thought, looked impossible. To have any chance of success he would have to be strong when he started.

Somehow he had to get inside the plane. All openings, even the small rear cargo hatch, were underwater so he couldn't get at them without diving and coming up inside the plane.

Where he would be trapped.

▶ What bothers Brian about the thought of being inside the plane?

He shuddered at that thought and then remembered what was in the front of the plane, down in the bottom of the lake, still strapped in the seat, the body of the pilot. Sitting there in the water—Brian could see him, the big man with his hair waving in the current, his eyes open . . .

Stop, he thought. Stop now. Stop that thinking. He was nearly at the point of swimming back to shore and forgetting the whole thing. But the image of the survival pack kept him. If he could get it out of the plane, or if he could just get into it and pull something out. A candy bar.

Even that—just a candy bar. It would be worth it.

But how to get at the inside of the plane?

He rolled off the raft and pulled himself around the plane. No openings. Three times he put his face in the water and opened his eyes and looked down. The water was murky, but he could see perhaps six feet and there was no obvious way to get into the plane. He was blocked.

Chapter 18

Brian worked around the tail of the plane two more times, pulling himself along on the stabilizer and the elevator, but there simply wasn't a way in.

Stupid, he thought. I was stupid to think I could just come out here and get inside the plane. Nothing is that easy. Not out here, not in this place. Nothing is easy.

He slammed his fist against the body of the plane and to his complete surprise the aluminum covering gave easily under his blow. He hit it again, and once more it bent and gave and he found that even when he didn't strike it but just pushed, it still moved. It was really, he thought, very thin aluminum skin over a kind of skeleton and if it gave that easily he might be able to force his way through . . .

The hatchet. He might be able to cut or hack with the hatchet. He reached to his belt and pulled the hatchet out, picked a place where the aluminum gave to his push and took an experimental swing at it.

The hatchet cut through the aluminum as if it were soft cheese. He couldn't believe it. Three more hacks and he had a triangular hole the size of his hand and he could see four cables that he guessed were the control cables going back to the tail and he hit the skin of the plane with a

◀ *How does Brian's frustration help him in this case?*

<u>frenzied</u> series of hacks to make a still larger opening and he was bending a piece of aluminum away from two aluminum braces of some kind when he dropped the hatchet.

It went straight down past his legs. He felt it bump his foot and then go on down, down into the water and for a second he couldn't understand that he had done it. For all this time, all the living and fighting, the hatchet had been everything—he had always worn it. Without the hatchet he had nothing—no fire, no tools, no weapons—he was nothing. The hatchet was, had been him.

And he had dropped it.

"Arrrgghhh!" He yelled it, choked on it, a snarl-cry of rage at his own carelessness. The hole in the plane was still too small to use for anything and now he didn't have a tool.

"That was the kind of thing I would have done before," he said to the lake, to the sky, to the trees. "When I came here—I would have done that. Not now. Not now . . ."

Yet he had and he hung on the raft for a moment and felt sorry for himself. For his own stupidity. But as before, the self-pity didn't help and he knew that he had only one course of action.

He had to get the hatchet back. He had to dive and get it back.

But how deep was it? In the deep end of the gym pool at school he had no trouble getting to the bottom and that was, he was pretty sure, about eleven feet.

Here it was impossible to know the exact depth. The front end of the plane, anchored by the weight of the engine, was obviously on the bottom but it came back up at an angle so the water wasn't as deep as the plane was long.

He pulled himself out of the water so his chest could expand, took two deep breaths and swiveled

▶ Why is Brian upset to lose the hatchet?

▶ What does Brian have to do?

words for everyday use

fren • zied (fren′ zēd) *adj.*, marked by wild agitation or movement. *The frenzied flailing of Gray's arms caught the attention of a passing motorist.*

and dove, pulling his arms and kicking off the raft bottom with his feet.

His first thrust took him down a good eight feet but the visibility was only five feet beyond that and he could not see bottom yet. He clawed down six or seven more feet, the pressure pushing in his ears until he held his nose and popped them and just as he ran out of breath and headed back up he thought he saw the bottom—still four feet below his dive.

He exploded out of the surface, bumping his head on the side of the elevator when he came up and took air like a whale, pushing the stale air out until he wheezed, taking new in. He would have to get deeper yet and still have time to search while he was down there.

Stupid, he thought once more, cursing himself—just dumb. He pulled air again and again, pushing his chest out until he could not possibly get any more capacity, then took one more deep lungful, wheeled and dove again.

This time he made an arrow out of his arms and used his legs to push off the bottom of the raft, all he had in his legs, to spring-snap and propel him down. As soon as he felt himself slowing a bit he started raking back with his arms at his sides, like paddles, and thrusting with his legs like a frog and this time he was so successful that he ran his face into the bottom mud.

He shook his head to clear his eyes and looked around. The plane disappeared out and down in front of him. He thought he could see the windows and that made him think again of the pilot sitting inside and he forced his thoughts from it—but he could see no hatchet. Bad air triggers were starting to go off in his brain and he knew he was limited to seconds now but he held for a moment and tried moving out a bit and just as he ran out of air, knew that he was going to have to blow soon, he saw the handle sticking out of the mud. He made one grab, missed, reached again and felt his fingers close on the rubber. He clutched it and in one motion slammed his feet down into the mud and powered himself up. But now his lungs were ready to explode and he had flashes of color in his brain, explosions of color, and he would have to take a pull of water, take it into his lungs and just as he opened his mouth to take it in, to pull in all the water in the lake his head blew out of the surface and into the light.

"*Tchaaak!*" It was as if a balloon had exploded. Old air blew out of his nose and mouth and he pulled new in again and again. He reached for the side of the raft and hung there, just breathing, until he could think once more—the hatchet clutched and shining in his right hand.

"All right . . . the plane. Still the plane . . ."

▶ Why is it slow going as Brian opens up the hole in the plane?

He went back to the hole in the fuselage and began to chop and cut again, peeling the aluminum skin off in pieces. It was slow going because he was careful, very careful with the hatchet, but he hacked and pulled until he had opened a hole large enough to pull his head and shoulders in and look down into the water. It was very dark inside the fuselage and he could see nothing—certainly no sign of the survival pack. There were some small pieces and bits of paper floating on the surface inside the plane—dirt from the floor of the plane that had floated up—but nothing <u>substantial</u>.

Well, he thought. Did you expect it to be easy? So easy that way? Just open her up and get the pack—right?

He would have to open it more, much more so he could poke down inside and see what he could find. The survival pack had been a zippered nylon bag, or perhaps canvas of some kind, and he thought it had been red, or was it gray? Well, that didn't matter. It must have been moved when the plane crashed and it might be jammed down under something else.

▶ Why does Brian save the bits he cuts out of the plane?

He started chopping again, cutting the aluminum away in small triangles, putting each one on the raft as he chopped—he could never throw anything away again, he thought—because they might be useful later. Bits of metal, fish arrowheads or lures, maybe.

---

words for everyday use

sub • stan • tial (səb stan′ chəl) *adj.*, considerable in quantity. *The <u>substantial</u> Thanksgiving meal kept the family full for hours.*

And when he finally finished again he had cleaned away the whole side and top of the fuselage that stuck out of the water, had cut down into the water as far as he could reach and had a hole almost as big as he was, except that it was crossed and crisscrossed with aluminum—or it might be steel, he couldn't tell—braces and formers[1] and cables. It was an awful tangled mess, but after chopping some braces away there was room for him to wiggle through and get inside.

He held back for a moment, uncomfortable with the thought of getting inside the plane. What if the tail settled back to the bottom and he got caught and couldn't get out? It was a horrible thought. But then he reconsidered. The thing had been up now for two days, plus a bit, and he had been hammering and climbing on it and it hadn't gone back down. It seemed pretty solid.

◄ How does Brian calm his fears about entering the plane?

He eeled in through the cables and formers, wiggling and pulling until he was inside the tail with his head clear of the surface of the water and his legs down on the angled floor. When he was ready, he took a deep breath and pushed down along the floor with his legs, feeling for some kind of fabric or cloth—anything—with his bare feet. He touched nothing but the floor plates.

Up, a new breath, then he reached down to formers underwater and pulled himself beneath the water, his legs pushing down and down almost to the backs of the front seats and finally, on the left side of the plane, he thought he felt his foot hit cloth or canvas.

Up for more air, deep breathing, then one more grab at the formers and pushing as hard as he could he jammed his feet down and he hit it again, definitely canvas or heavy nylon, and this time when he pushed his foot he thought he felt something inside it; something hard.

It had to be the bag. Driven forward by the crash, it was jammed into the backs of the seats and caught

---

1. **braces and formers.** Structural parts of an airplane, such as support beams and walls

on something. He tried to reach for it and pull but didn't have the air left and went up for more.

Lungs filled in great gulps, he shot down again, pulling on the formers until he was almost there, then wheeling down head first he grabbed at the cloth. It was the survival bag. He pulled and tore at it to loosen it and just as it broke free and his heart leaped to feel it rise he looked up, above the bag. In the light coming through the side window, the pale green light from the water, he saw the pilot's head only it wasn't the pilot's head any longer.

The fish. He'd never really thought of it, but the fish—the fish he had been eating all this time had to eat, too. They had been at the pilot all this time, almost two months, nibbling and chewing and all that remained was the not quite cleaned skull and when he looked up it wobbled loosely.

Too much. Too much. His mind screamed in horror and he slammed back and was sick in the water, sick so that he choked on it and tried to breathe water and could have ended there, ended with the pilot where it almost ended when they first arrived except that his legs jerked. It was instinctive, fear more than anything else, fear of what he had seen. But they jerked and pushed and he was headed up when they jerked and he shot to the surface, still inside the birdcage of formers and cables.

His head slammed into a bracket as he cleared and he reached up to grab it and was free, in the air, hanging up in the tail.

He hung that way for several minutes, choking and heaving and gasping for air, fighting to clear the picture of the pilot from his mind. It went slowly— he knew it would never completely leave—but he looked to the shore and there were trees and birds, the sun was getting low and golden over his shelter and when he stopped coughing he could hear the gentle sounds of evening, the peace sounds, the bird sounds and the breeze in the trees.

The peace finally came to him and he settled his breathing. He was still a long way from being finished—had a lot of work to do. The bag was floating

▶ What does Brian see just as he is about to free the bag?

next to him but he had to get it out of the plane and onto the raft, then back to shore.

He wiggled out through the formers—it seemed harder than when he came in—and pulled the raft around. The bag fought him. It was almost as if it didn't want to leave the plane. He pulled and jerked and still it wouldn't fit and at last he had to change the shape of it, rearranging what was inside by pushing and pulling at the sides until he had narrowed it and made it longer. Even when it finally came it was difficult and he had to pull first at one side, then another, an inch at a time, squeezing it through.

◀ What difficulties does Brian face after he finds the bag?

All of this took some time and when he finally got the bag out and tied on top of the raft it was nearly dark, he was bone tired from working in the water all day, chilled deep, and he still had to push the raft to shore.

Many times he thought he would not make it. With the added weight of the bag—which seemed to get heavier by the foot—coupled with the fact that he was getting weaker all the time, the raft seemed barely to move. He kicked and pulled and pushed, taking the shortest way straight back to shore, hanging to rest many times, then surging again and again.

It seemed to take forever and when at last his feet hit bottom and he could push against the mud and slide the raft into the shore weeds to bump against the bank he was so weak he couldn't stand, had to crawl; so tired he didn't even notice the mosquitos that tore into him like a gray, angry cloud.

He had done it.

That's all he could think now. He had done it.

◀ What does Brian think as he reaches the shore?

He turned and sat on the bank with his legs in the water and pulled the bag ashore and began the long drag—he couldn't lift it—back down the shoreline to his shelter. Two hours, almost three he dragged and stumbled in the dark, brushing the mosquitos away, sometimes on his feet, more often on his knees, finally to drop across the bag and to sleep when he made the sand in front of the doorway.

He had done it.

Chapter 19

▶ How does Brian
feel at first about
what he finds in the
survival pack?

Treasure.

Unbelievable riches. He could not believe the contents of the survival pack.

The night before he was so numb with exhaustion he couldn't do anything but sleep. All day in the water had tired him so much that, in the end, he had fallen asleep sitting against his shelter wall, <u>oblivious</u> even to the mosquitos, to the night, to anything. But with false gray dawn he had awakened instantly, and began to dig in the pack—to find amazing, wonderful things.

There was a sleeping bag—which he hung to dry over his shelter roof on the outside—and foam sleeping pad. An aluminum cookset with four little pots and two frying pans; it actually even had a fork and knife and spoon. A waterproof container with matches and two small butane lighters. A sheath knife with a compass in the handle: As if a compass would help him, he thought, smiling. A first-aid kit with bandages and tubes of antiseptic paste and small scissors. A cap that said CESSNA across the front in large letters. Why a cap? he wondered. It was adjustable and he put it on immediately. A fishing kit

**words
for
everyday
use**   ob • liv • i • ous (ə bliv′ ē əs) *adj.,* unaware, without knowledge. *When she walked into
class with her shirt on backward, Reshma was <u>oblivious</u> to her classmates' stares of disbelief.*

with four coils of line, a dozen small lures, and hooks and sinkers.

Incredible wealth. It was like all the holidays in the world, all the birthdays there were. He sat in the sun by the doorway where he had dropped the night before and pulled the presents—as he thought of them—out one at a time to examine them, turn them in the light, touch them and feel them with his hands and eyes.

Something that at first puzzled him. He pulled out what seemed to be the broken-off, bulky stock of a rifle and he was going to put it aside, thinking it might be for something else in the pack, when he shook it and it rattled. After working at it for a moment he found the butt of the stock came off and inside there was a barrel and magazine and action assembly, with a clip and a full box of fifty shells. It was a .22 survival rifle—he had seen one once in the sporting goods store where he went for bike parts— and the barrel screwed onto the stock. He had never owned a rifle, never fired one, but had seen them on television, of course, and after a few moments figured out how to put it together by screwing the action onto the stock, how to load it and put the clip full of bullets into the action.

It was a strange feeling, holding the rifle. It somehow removed him from everything around him. Without the rifle he had to fit in, to be part of it all, to understand it and use it—the woods, all of it. With the rifle, suddenly, he didn't have to know; did not have to be afraid or understand. He didn't have to get close to a foolbird to kill it—didn't have to know how it would stand if he didn't look at it and moved off to the side.

◀ What is Brian's reaction to finding the rifle and the lighter?

The rifle changed him, the minute he picked it up, and he wasn't sure he liked the change very much. He set it aside, leaning it carefully against the wall. He could deal with that feeling later. The fire was out and he used a butane lighter and a piece of birchbark with small twigs to get another one started—marveling at how easy it was but feeling again that the lighter somehow removed him from where he was, what he had to know. With a ready flame he didn't have to know how to make a spark nest, or how to feed the new flames to make them grow. As with the rifle, he wasn't sure he liked the change.

Up and down, he thought. The pack was wonderful but it gave him up and down feelings.

With the fire going and sending up black smoke and a steady roar from a pitch-smelling chunk he put on, he turned once more to the pack. Rummaging through the food packets—he hadn't brought them out yet because he wanted to save them until last, glory in them—he came up with a small electronic device completely encased in a plastic bag. At first he thought it was a radio or cassette player and he had a surge of hope because he missed music, missed sound, missed hearing another voice. But when he opened the plastic and took the thing out and turned it over he could see that it wasn't a receiver at all. There was a coil of wire held together on the side by tape and it sprung into a three foot long antenna when he took the tape off. No speaker, no lights, just a small switch at the top and on the bottom he finally found, in small print.

▶ What does Brian think about the emergency transmitter?

Emergency Transmitter.

That was it. He turned the switch back and forth a few times but nothing happened—he couldn't even hear static—so, as with the rifle, he set it against the wall and went back to the bag. It was probably ruined in the crash, he thought.

Two bars of soap.

He had bathed regularly in the lake, but not with soap and he thought how wonderful it would be to wash his hair. Thick with grime and smoke dirt, frizzed by wind and sun, matted with fish and fool-bird grease, his hair had grown and stuck and tangled and grown until it was a clumped mess on his head. He could use the scissors from the first-aid kit to cut it off, then wash it with soap.

And then, finally—the food.

It was all freeze-dried and in such quantity that he thought, With this I could live forever. Package after package he took out, beef dinner with potatoes, cheese and noodle dinners, chicken dinners, egg and potato breakfasts, fruit mixes, drink mixes, dessert mixes, more dinners and breakfasts than he could count easily, dozens and dozens of them all packed in waterproof bags, all in perfect shape and when he had them all out and laid against the wall in stacks he couldn't stand it and he went through them again.

If I'm careful, he thought, they'll last as long as . . . as long as I need them to last. If I'm careful. . . . No. Not yet. I won't be careful just yet. First I am going to have a feast. Right here and now I am going to cook up a feast and eat until I drop and then I'll be careful.

◄ How long will the food last if Brian is careful?

He went into the food packs once more and selected what he wanted for his feast: a four-person beef and potato dinner, with orange drink for an appetizer and something called a peach whip for dessert. Just add water, it said on the packages, and cook for half an hour or so until everything was normal-size and done.

Brian went to the lake and got water in one of the aluminum pots and came back to the fire. Just that amazed him—to be able to carry water to the fire in a pot. Such a simple act and he hadn't been able to do it for almost two months. He guessed at the amounts and put the beef dinner and peach dessert on to boil, then went back to the lake and brought water to mix with the orange drink.

◄ What simple act amazes Brian?

It was sweet and tangy—almost too sweet—but so good that he didn't drink it fast, held it in his mouth and let the taste go over his tongue. Tickling on the sides, sloshing it back and forth and then down, swallow, then another.

That, he thought, that is just fine. Just fine. He got more lake water and mixed another one and drank it fast, then a third one, and he sat with that near the fire but looking out across the lake, thinking how rich the smell was from the cooking beef dinner. There was garlic in it and some other spices and the smells came up to him and made him think of home, his mother cooking, the rich smells of the kitchen, and at that precise instant, with his mind full of home and the smell from the food filling him, the plane appeared.

He had only a moment of warning. There was a tiny drone but as before it didn't register, then suddenly, roaring over his head low and in back of the ridge a bushplane with floats fairly exploded into his life.

It passed directly over him, very low, tipped a wing sharply over the tail of the crashed plane in the lake, cut power, glided down the long part of the L of the lake, then turned and glided back, touching the water gently once, twice, and settling with a spray to taxi[1] and stop with its floats gently bumping the beach in front of Brian's shelter.

▶ How does Brian react at first to seeing the plane?

He had not moved. It had all happened so fast that he hadn't moved. He sat with the pot of orange drink still in his hand, staring at the plane, not quite understanding it yet; not quite knowing yet that it was over.

The pilot cut the engine, opened the door, and got out, balanced, and stepped forward on the float to hop onto the sand without getting his feet wet. He was wearing sunglasses and he took them off to stare at Brian.

"I heard your emergency transmitter—then I saw the plane when I came over . . ." He trailed off, cocked his head, studying Brian. "Damn. You're him, aren't you? You're that kid. They quit looking, a month, no, almost two months ago. You're him, aren't you? You're that kid . . ."

Brian was standing now, but still silent, still holding the drink. His tongue seemed to be stuck to the roof of his mouth and his throat didn't work right. He looked at the pilot, and the plane, and down at himself—dirty and ragged, burned and lean and tough—and he coughed to clear his throat.

▶ What does Brian say to the pilot?

"My name is Brian Robeson," he said. Then he saw that his stew was done, the peach whip almost done, and he waved to it with his hand. "Would you like something to eat?"

---

1. **taxi.** Go at low speed along land or water

Epilogue

The pilot who landed so suddenly in the lake was a fur buyer mapping Cree trapping camps for future buying runs—drawn by Brian when he unwittingly turned on the emergency transmitter and left it going. The Cree move into the camps for fall and winter to trap and the buyers fly from camp to camp on a regular route.

◄ How did the pilot find Brian?

When the pilot rescued Brian he had been alone on the L-shaped lake for fifty-four days. During that time he had lost seventeen percent of his body weight. He later gained back six percent, but had virtually no body fat—his body had consumed all extra weight and he would remain lean and wiry for several years.

Many of the changes would prove to be permanent. Brian had gained immensely in his ability to observe what was happening and react to it; that would last him all his life. He had become more thoughtful as well, and from that time on he would think slowly about something before speaking.

◄ What are two of the major changes in Brian?

Food, all food, even food he did not like, never lost its wonder for him. For years after his rescue he would find himself stopping in grocery stores to just stare at the aisles of food, marveling at the quantity and the variety.

There were many questions in his mind about what he had seen and known, and he worked at research when he got back, identifying the game and berries.

◄ How does Brian learn about the plants and animals he saw in the wilderness?

Gut cherries were termed choke cherries, and made good jelly. The nut bushes where the foolbirds hid were hazelnut bushes. The two kinds of rabbits were snowshoes and cottontails; the foolbirds were ruffed grouse (also called fool hens by trappers, for their stupidity); the small food fish were bluegills, sunfish, and perch; the turtle eggs were laid by a snapping turtle, as he had thought; the wolves were timber wolves, which are not known to attack or bother people; the moose was a moose.

There were also the dreams—he had many dreams about the lake after he was rescued. The Canadian government sent a team in to recover the body of the pilot and they took reporters, who naturally took pictures and film of the whole campsite, the shelter—all of it. For a brief time the press made much of Brian and he was interviewed for several networks but the <u>furor</u> died within a few months. A writer showed up who wanted to do a book on the "complete adventure" (as he called it) but he turned out to be a dreamer and it all came to nothing but talk. Still Brian was given copies of the pictures and tape, and looking at them seemed to trigger the dreams. They were not nightmares, none of them were frightening, but he would awaken at times with them; just awaken and sit up and think of the lake, the forest, the fire at night, the night birds singing, the fish jumping—sit in the dark alone and think of them and it was not bad and would never be bad for him.

Predictions are, for the most part, ineffective; but it might be interesting to note that had Brian not been rescued when he was, had he been forced to go into hard fall, perhaps winter, it would have been very rough on him. When the lake froze he would have lost the fish, and when the snow got deep he would have had trouble moving at all. Game becomes seemingly plentiful in the fall (it's easier to see with the leaves off the brush) but in winter it gets

▶ What kinds of dreams does Brian have about his time in the wilderness?

▶ What difficulties would Brian have faced had he not been rescued?

scarce and sometimes simply nonexistent as predators (fox, lynx, wolf, owls, weasels, fisher, martin, northern coyote) sweep through areas and wipe things out. It is amazing what a single owl can do to a local population of ruffed grouse and rabbits in just a few months.

After the initial surprise and happiness from his parents at his being alive—for a week it looked as if they might actually get back together—things rapidly went back to normal. His father returned to the northern oil fields, where Brian eventually visited him, and his mother stayed in the city, worked at her career in real estate, and continued to see the man in the station wagon.

Brian tried several times to tell his father, came really close once to doing it, but in the end never said a word about the man or what he knew, the Secret.

◀ *What does Brian do about the Secret?*

Respond to the Selection

If you were a reporter who had the chance to interview Brian, what questions would you ask him? How do you think he would answer your questions?

Investigate, Inquire, and Imagine

Recall: Gather Facts

1a. Why does Brian decide to go back to the plane? What happens to the hatchet while he is trying to get into the plane?

2a. What does Brian see in the plane when he is underwater?

3a. Who rescues Brian?

Interpret: Find Meaning

1b. Why does it take Brian so long to get into the plane? Why is all of his effort worthwhile?

2b. How does he feel about what he sees?

3b. How does Brian react to being rescued?

Analyze: Take Things Apart

4a. How does Brian feel about the things he finds in the survival pack? Why does he have mixed feelings?

Synthesize: Bring Things Together

4b. How would Brian's experience have been different if he had found the survival pack earlier?

Evaluate: Make Judgments

5a. How important was the Secret to this story? Why do you think the author included it?

Extend: Connect Ideas

5b. Do you think Brian's feelings about the Secret changed since the beginning of the story? If so, why might they have changed? Why do you think Brian chose not to tell his father about the Secret?

Understanding Literature

RESOLUTION AND DÉNOUEMENT. The **resolution** is the point in the plot of a story or play at which the central conflict is ended or resolved. The **dénouement** is any material that follows the resolution and that ties up loose ends. What are the resolution and dénouement of *Hatchet*?

CHARACTER AND CHARACTERIZATION. A **character** is a person (or sometimes an animal) who takes part in the action of a literary work. **Characterization** is the act of creating a character. Writers create characters using three major techniques: showing what characters say, do, or think; showing what other characters say or think about them; and by describing the physical features, dress, and personality of the character. Review the notes you took earlier about the character of Brian and the techniques Paulsen used to create this character. How has Brian changed over the course of the novel? How do you know? What techniques does Paulsen use to create the "new" Brian?

Plot Analysis of
Hatchet

A **plot** is a series of events related to a **central conflict,** or struggle. The following plot pyramid illustrates the main parts of a plot.

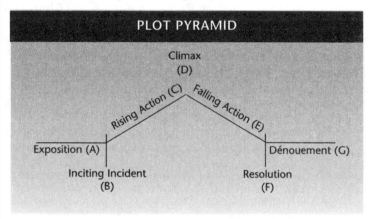

The parts of a plot are as follows:

The **exposition** is the part of a plot that provides the background information, often about the characters, setting, or conflict.

The **inciting incident** is the event that introduces the central conflict.

The **rising action**, or complication, develops the conflict to a high point of intensity.

The **climax** is the high point of interest or suspense in the plot.

The **falling action** is all of the events that follow the climax.

The **resolution** is the point at which the central conflict is ended, or resolved.

The **dénouement** is any material that follows the resolution and that ties up any loose ends.

Exposition (A)

The reader learns that Brian Robeson, a thirteen-year-old boy, is on a small plane headed to Canada. He is going to visit his father, who is working in the Canadian oil fields. Brian's parents are divorced and Brian's father has visiting rights during the summer.

Brian is very unhappy about the divorce and, especially, about the Secret. The secret is mentioned, but the reader does not know what it is.

Inciting Incident (B)

The pilot has a heart attack and dies while flying the plane. Before he dies, he accidentally pushes the plane off course. Brian has to fly the plane. He radios for help but gets cut off. He is afraid to land the plane, but once it runs out of gas, he has to figure out a way to bring the plane down. He survives a crash landing on a lake, escapes the sinking aircraft, and swims to shore. The story centers on Brian's efforts to survive alone in the wilderness after the crash.

Rising Action (C)

Brian starts to deal with his needs. He builds a shelter, learns to make fire, and discovers ways to find food. None of these things come easily to Brian. During this time, he struggles to keep up his hope. He also has some problems, such as being attacked by a porcupine and sprayed by a skunk.

Climax, Crisis/Turning Point (D)

While Brian is busy getting food, he hears a plane. He rushes back to light his signal fire, but the plane turns away without seeing the fire. As the plane flies off, Brian loses hope of ever being rescued. Brian has a dark night of crying, lets his fire go out, and tries to put an end to his misery. He comes through these events as a stronger person, ready to do whatever it takes to survive.

Falling Action (E)

Brian continues to build his survival skills. A moose attacks and injures him. A tornado rips through the area, destroying his shelter, fish pond, and fire. He must rebuild his life. Surprisingly, the tornado also moves the plane wreck to the surface. With difficulty, Brian gets the survival pack out of the plane. In it he finds matches, weapons, a sleeping bag, and food. He has mixed feelings about what he finds. He realizes that if he had had these things at the beginning, he would not have understood his environment as well. Learning to pay attention and be part of the environment helped him learn to survive. In the survival pack, Brian also finds an emergency transmitter. He thinks it is broken because it doesn't do anything when he tries to turn it on.

Resolution (F)

A bush pilot hears the signal from the emergency transmitter. He finds Brian and rescues him.

Dénouement (G)

The epilogue provides the dénouement. There is a lot of news coverage of Brian's ordeal. He hopes his parents will get back together, but they do not.

"Walking on the Jornada del Muerto Desert"
from *Finding Your Way: The Art of Natural Navigation* by Jennifer Owings Dewey

ABOUT THE RELATED READING

Jennifer Owings Dewey is a naturalist, author, and children's book illustrator who lives in Santa Fe, New Mexico. In this story, she describes a time when she had to walk out of the desert when her truck broke an axle—a very dangerous walk, considering the dry and desolate landscape. In fact, the name of the desert—Jornada del Muerto—means "journey of the dead man." This story was published in Dewey's book *Finding Your Way: The Art of Natural Navigation* (2001).

"It's not on any map—no true places ever are."

—*Mark Twain*

There are no roads in the Jornada, only cow trails studded with tire-popping volcanic rocks. I wrestled a four-wheel-drive vehicle across this rough, dry desert in New Mexico for seventy miles, the only sign of human presence an occasional windmill, a slender <u>sentinel</u> breaking the <u>monotony</u> of the nearly flat landscape. Rusty stock tanks riddled with bullet holes squat near the bottoms of the windmills, the slimy water surface buzzing with insects.

I came alone to the lava flats in the desert. I wanted to explore a cave where a colony of Mexican freetail bats, all females, spends the summer raising bat babies. A biologist friend who had been to the cave <u>scrawled</u> directions for me, and I set off.

◀ *Why did Dewey go to the desert?*

| words for everyday use | **sen • ti • nel** (sent' ə nəl) *n.*, guard. *My dog is a <u>sentinel</u>; he warns my family by barking whenever anyone approaches our house.* | **mo • not • o • ny** (mə nät' ən ē) *n.*, same to the point of being tedious. *The arrival of an unexpected guest broke the <u>monotony</u> of Lila's days.* |

After reaching the cave, I spent the afternoon and evening crawling around in the <u>cavity</u> that is home to the bats. The cave air is <u>rank</u> with the stench of ammonia from bat urine and hazy from shed fur. Baby bats slip silently to the cave floor, to be devoured in minutes by dermestid beetles.[1]

I left the cave early the next morning. Shortly after starting for the highway, an uneven rut threw my truck into a boulder. The axle was broken.

I stood paralyzed by the ruined truck, flooded with disbelief at what had happened. I was stranded and would have to walk out on foot. A wind like hot stale breath pushed against me. I wanted to cry out, "Don't leave me all alone out here!"

I tried to focus on where I was. Because I was on foot I could strike north, a shortcut impossible with the truck. I hoped to intersect the main road, a distance of about fifty miles.

Two distant mountain ranges, one in the east, another in the west, helped me figure direction. I knew if I walked between the two ranges I would be going north. If I made the mistake of turning south I would face many miles of waterless desert clear into Mexico.

For hours, until it collapsed in the dirt, I followed a fence line, droopy strands of barbed wire stapled to weathered posts. To save energy I went slowly and stopped often. My head swirled with doubts about surviving the July heat with half a canteen of water. Alone and scared, I was struck by the immense loneliness of desert space and silence.

I said prayers for survival and prayers that I'd have sense enough to keep north and not go in circles.

▶ What problem did Dewey face? How far would she have to walk?

▶ What doubts did Dewey have?

---

1. **dermestid beetles.** Small, drab-colored beetles that eat animals and animal products

---

Desert heat adds to a traveler's confusion by creating mirages.[2] I thought I saw mountain ranges covered with snow, pools of bright blue water, sea waves, images floating in the distance that looked real but were vapor, not real at all.

◀ What is a mirage?

A pattern of sound penetrated my brain, a symphony of noises from desert-dwelling animals. Gradually I began to notice what was happening around me.

◀ What did Dewey begin to notice as she walked?

Black grasshoppers bumped against my legs and ankles, fat green flies buzzed like heavy bombers on dark wings, white moths fluttered over dry stems. A wasp dove for a red ant closing in on a tiny beetle running for its life.

I became obsessed with <u>minutiae</u>. Focusing on tiny things helped clear my mind. A tarantula walked on the sand, leaving a delicate trail of claw marks in its wake. The spider lifted hairy legs and set them down with ballet-like precision. I brushed the tarantula's back with a cactus spine. It hesitated, then went on. The indifference of the tarantula to my pestering was oddly reassuring.

A snake of a species unknown to me slipped by. Rosy-scaled and skinny as a rope, it seemed to <u>levitate</u> over the ground and not touch down.

"Where are you going?" I asked. "If you're headed for water, take me with you."

I gently poked a carrion beetle[3] with a twig of sagebrush. Two inches long, with smooth, shiny wing covers, it reacted by standing on its head. I gently knocked it over, and it righted itself. Whether the

---

2. **mirage.** A mirage is an illusion created when light rays pass from one layer of air to another, one layer cold, another warm. The speed of the passing light rays is altered, and the rays are bent (refracted) so they strike the eye from a direction different from their point of origin. Light rays passing through layers of air often create shimmering pools of blue, even on sunbaked pavement, giving the impression of water where none exists. [Explanation taken from a photo caption in *Finding Your Way*.]

3. **carrion beetle.** A type of beetle that feeds off the carcasses of dead animals

---

words for everyday use

mi • nu • tiae (mi nü′ shē ē′) *n. pl.,* minor details. *Ne focuses on <u>minutiae</u>, while Raisa focuses on the big picture.*

lev • i • tate (lev′ ə tāt) *v.,* rise or float in the air. *The magician's assistant appeared to <u>levitate</u> over the table.*

beetle knew which trail to take, it knew where to put its clawed feet.

I thought of how the first human travelers in the desert had found their way across windswept dunes from one oasis[4] to the next. Ancient traders surely used the sun by day, and the stars by night, establishing long-lasting trade routes. I looked for game trails running north. Small herds of antelope cross the Jornada, following often, if not always, the shortest routes.

▶ On what did Dewey waste energy?

Any true sense of where I was in space and time was <u>distorted</u> by my fear. I panicked and lost north and had to stop and locate it again. I wasted good energy being angry. The stony, cactus-strewn land made me furious. I was no match for the harsh country, not tough enough. My lips, tongue, and throat were swollen from thirst, my skin bright red, blistered by the sun.

I scared up a covey of quail.[5] They buzzed away with top-knot feathers quivering, horrified at being caught in the open, startled by a <u>looming</u> intruder. The little birds seemed too delicate for the desert, fragile and soft in contrast to the harsh landscape. I thought of my own obvious fragility.

▶ What kinds of physical discomfort does a person face when lost in a desert?

It is impossible to imagine what being stranded and "lost" feels like. Exhaustion makes you wonder how your legs are going to keep you standing, to say nothing of walking. Every joint aches. Hunger makes you stagger. Thirst makes you want to create moisture in your mouth, but you can't produce any saliva.

A beetle trail and the prints of a kangaroo rat marked a patch of sand. These animals never drink. All the moisture they need is in their food. They rarely urinate, excreting tiny, brownish, concentrated droplets three or four times in their lives.

---

4. **oasis.** Green area of plant life in a desert, often centered around water
5. **covey of quail.** Flock of small, short-tailed birds

words for everyday use

dis • tort (di stôrt') v., twisted out of proportion or natural shape. *Adam's face was distorted as he winced in pain.*

loom • ing (lüm' iŋ) adj., taking shape as an approaching object, often appearing larger than life or in distorted form. *The looming clouds made it clear that a storm was fast approaching.*

After many hours of walking, I began to "see" leaping, charging snakes and a dancer with feathers on his head, and I knew I was hallucinating, suffering the early stages of heat stroke. I found a patch of shade and took a nap.

◀ Why did Dewey stop to take a nap?

When I was up and moving again, I thought: Antelope and coyote live out here, why not me, for a few hours at least?

"Just passing through," I said, addressing a brittle shaft of ocatilla.[6]

My feet kicked up dry seedpods with weird shapes, containers for new life. One looked like a miniature goat's head with prickly spines. Dry brown grass leaned away from the wind, falling on the ground like strands of hair. The grass looked defeated, and I could not imagine it ever being green.

I yearned for rain, and knew by the bright, cloudless sky that none was in the making. Westerlies, the <u>prevailing</u> winds, brought only warm air blowing over the ground.

Toward evening Swainson's hawks appeared in the sky. I became tearfully awash (dry tears) with admiration and envy. If you are a hawk and take a notion to fly fifteen miles to water you do—simple as that.

◀ Why did Dewey admire and envy the hawks?

Dark shadows grew across the land, and the western horizon turned pink and blue. A thick brown haze, the last of a far-off dust storm, drifted like smoke. Fire-red clouds lit by the sun's last light promised relief from the heat.

When the moon was high, the night turned cold. I scratched out a spot and burrowed into the sand like a horned lizard seeking warmth.

Morning came with the calls of doves, low and soft, like women weeping in a graveyard. I woke up amazed to have slept. Butterflies were everywhere in the heavy, warm air.

---

6. **ocatilla.** A type of cactus, also called ocotillo or candlewood

words for everyday use   **pre • vail • ing** (pri vā′ liŋ) *adj.*, most frequent or common. *Uma is one of the minority who disagrees with the <u>prevailing</u> opinion.*

▶ Why was Dewey
hopeful when she
spotted a windmill?

▶ What could Dewey
see from the top of
the windmill
platform?

▶ How did she feel
abou leaving the
desert?

I set off north and saw a windmill ahead. Windmills mean a chance of water.

A scummy water hole surrounded the base of the windmill, leakage from the tank. I dared not drink.

A metal ladder was bolted to the rusted legs of the windmill. I climbed to the top, sat on a rickety platform of weathered wood, and looked north. The two-lane paved highway was visible in the distance. I knew that I would reach it before falling face down dead of thirst and heat in the sand.

Standing at the roadside, I felt a pang of sadness at leaving the desert. So much of my time had been <u>consumed</u> in feeling angry and afraid. I'd missed chances to <u>revel</u> in the experience. I wished I could go back and do it over, do it right.

A car whooshed past and screeched to a halt. It backed up and stopped where I stood. A woman in a tattered straw hat and a pretty summer dress was behind the wheel. She had the windows open. Dust swirled inside the car like sea fog.

"You are *filthy*," she said, staring at me. "You been living underground?"

She took me to town, where I drank gallons of lemonade and had an endless bath before finding someone to help me rescue my truck.

Critical Thinking

1. What kinds of physical and mental difficulties did Jennifer Owings Dewey need to overcome to get out of the desert? Compare and contrast her needs to Brian's needs in the Canadian wilderness.
2. Compare Dewey's observations about anger with Brian's observations about self-pity.
3. What kinds of things did Dewey begin to notice as she walked through the desert? How did paying attention to her environment help her?
4. How did Dewey feel about leaving the desert? Why? How do you think you would react in her situation?

---

words for everyday use

con • sume (kən süm') v., use up, waste. *Homework consumes too much of my time.*

rev • el (rev' əl) v., take pleasure or satisfaction. *During the summer, Rudy reveled in his freedom to sleep late in the morning and play outside all afternoon.*

"Castaway Challenge"
Teen Spends 48 Hours Alone on Island
by Thomas E. Goldstone
abcnews.com

ABOUT THE RELATED READING

"Castaway Challenge" describes the real-life experience of Caroline, a seventeen-year-old girl who spent two days alone on an island off the coast of Maine. The experience helped Caroline to become more confident and independent.

Aug. 22—Caroline, a 17-year-old who asked that her last name not be used, has always feared being home alone.

When the walls of her Connecticut house creaked, she was told as a little girl, it was the ghost of a Revolutionary War general groaning.

And it wasn't just her home that petrified her. She just wasn't very good at being alone anywhere.

Despite her fear—actually, precisely *because* of her fear—Caroline signed up for a program where after almost a week of sea kayaking, she would have to spend 48 hours alone in the wilderness of Maine, in what the Hurricane Island Outward Bound School[1] calls "a solo."

◄ Why did Caroline sign up for the solo wilderness experience? How long would she have to spend on the island?

"I did it to be comfortable with being alone," she says.

Roughing It

Caroline was given a duffel bag in which to pack the few belongings she was allowed to bring: a sleeping bag, a tarp to make shelter, warm clothes and foul weather gear in case of rain, a whistle to blow should trouble strike, an apple, a piece of cheese, a limited amount of trail mix and plenty of water.

◄ What supplies did Caroline have for her stay? How did she feel when she was dropped off?

---

1. **Outward Bound School.** Program that focuses on personal growth through experiences, often in the wilderness

"This is really roughing it," says Caroline, who was dropped off on Two Bush Island, in Penobscott Bay in Maine. "You feel kind of <u>vulnerable</u>."

Instead of falling apart while confronting her worst fear, Caroline thrived. To keep herself company—and to document her life-changing experience—she wrote letters home and in her journal:

▶ What movie did Caroline's experience remind her of? What did she say ruled her world when on the island?

I feel like Tom Hanks on Cast Away. *I have my own private island . . . I feel vulnerable. There are waves crashing around me . . . I don't have an endless supply of food . . . There's no solid walls around me to break the strong wind . . . It's funny how when on land, my life is ruled by clocks. Now my life is sort of ruled by the sun.*

. . . My activities have mainly consisted of me shifting places and moving around the island. I might move because the sun is stronger on one side than the other . . . or I want to go into that special little nook which is perfect for an afternoon nap. I know the comfy spots now. Like where I'm well-sheltered from the wind, or where to sit for a perfect sunset. Certain sounds, which would have normally made my head turn, I ignore. Because I've gotten so used to them. Friday when I came, I was frightened by the high tide, but today I could comfortably sit on the east side without being scared or thinking about it at all.

A Life-Changing Experience

▶ What did Caroline see and hear on the last night of her solo?

On her last night, Caroline thought she heard thunder. At first she was frightened about what to do in case of rain. But when she poked her head out of her tent, she saw fireworks in the sky that were part of a summer celebration of a community across the bay.

"What a way to end my solo," she says.

And what a way to for a young woman to make a change in her life.

"How often can you say, 'Yeah, I was thrown on a

---

words for everyday use

vul • ner • a • ble (vuln' rə bəl *or* vul' nə rə bəl) *adj.*, open to attack or damage. *The soldiers knew that the <u>vulnerable</u> part of the fort was near the front entrance, where the walls were crumbling and too low.*

deserted island for two days'?" she says. "I think I'll be a little more independent now . . . because I know I can take care of myself . . . I have the capability to do anything if I set my mind to it."

◀ Overall, what effect did the experience have on Caroline?

Critical Thinking

1. How did Caroline feel about her experience on the island? How do you think Caroline's experience would have differed if her "solo" had been for a longer period of time?
2. Compare and contrast Caroline's solo on the island with Brian's experience in *Hatchet*.
3. What are the benefits and drawbacks to being alone? Use the experiences of Caroline and Brian as examples.
4. Would you want to do a "solo" like this? Why, or why not?

"Survival: Be Prepared. Be Aware. Stay Alive."
by Buck Tilton
from *Backpacker* magazine, August 2002

ABOUT THE RELATED READING

"Survival: Be Prepared. Be Aware. Stay Alive" shares advice from survivors and survival and rescue experts. The article describes traits, skills, and tools that are helpful to survivors. It emphasizes the importance of being prepared and offers guidance on what to do if you are lost or in a dangerous situation.

In 1992, Colby Coombs and two rope-mates slid 800 feet down Alaska's Mt. Foraker. His companions died; Coombs broke his neck, ankle, and shoulder blade. He hobbled 6 miles to the nearest ranger station, a journey that took him more than 5 days. How did he manage to survive? He didn't have a choice—not if he wanted to live. "And I did."

▶ *What two traits do survivors have?*

Survivors share two <u>traits</u>, according to Daryl Miller, the lead rescuer on Denali.[1] "They have confidence in their outdoors skills, and they start taking care of themselves instead of just sitting there and waiting on a rescue." Retired park ranger Charles "Butch" Farabee adds a third: "Ideals." Survivors "have family or friendship that give them the desire to live," says Farabee, a veteran of more than 1,000 SAR missions.

▶ *What are the four mistakes hikers often make that get them into trouble?*

Then there are the mistakes that get hikers in trouble in the first place. Farabee points to the deadly four: failing to imagine a worst-case scenario and prepare for it; ignoring the weather; failing to leave an <u>itinerary</u>; and overestimating one's abilities.

What should you do when you get in a fix? Read on.

---

1. **Denali.** The highest mountain in North America, also known as Mt. McKinley

---

words for everyday use
   trait (trāt) *n.*, distinguishing quality or characteristic. *Patience and self-confidence are positive character <u>traits</u>.*

GEAR TO DIE FOR

What's not in your kit could kill you.

SUPERGLUE

The knife went wild and the cut went deep. When you're days from medical care, search your pack for superglue. It can safely be used to hold skin shut as long as you keep the goo out of the wound. Just remember to irrigate the wound before holding it closed and gluing the surface shut.

◀ What are five objects that could save your life if you have them in your gear?

DRINKING STRAW

"On big climbs, I carry a plastic drinking straw in my suit. When there are little trickles of water on the rocks, I can drink," says Conrad Anker, Himalayan climber and Mallory's discoverer on Everest.[2] "Works on desert potholes, too."

PEE BOTTLE

In a cold-weather emergency, a full pee bottle can act as a hot water bottle. Use the urine's heat to keep warm for a couple of hours.

SUNGLASSES

Wearing sunglasses after dark limits the heat escaping through your eyes. "It can make a <u>perceptible</u> difference in body heat <u>retention</u>," says John Gookin, survival expert with NOLS [National Outdoor Leadership School].

DUCT TAPE

Use it to secure splints to broken limbs, craft avalanche probes, fashion an emergency shelter, and more.

---

2. **Mallory's discoverer on Everest.** George Mallory was lost in an attempt to climb Mt. Everest in 1924. A search team found his body in 1999.

words for everyday use

itin • er • ary (ī tin′ ə rer′ ē) *n.*, route or plan of a trip. *Our travel agent sent us an* *itinerary that included the arrival and departure time for each of our flights.*

per • cep • ti • ble (pər sep′ tə bəl) *adj.*, noticeable by the senses. *We noticed a* *perceptible difference in temperature when* *we moved our chairs to the shade.*

re • ten • tion (ri ten′ chən) *n.*, act of keeping or retaining. *We get people to join the club, but our rate of retention is low.*

DEADLY MISTAKES OF THE LOST

Don't try these tricks away from home.

Sometimes it's obvious. Your plane crash lands just north of nowhere, and you look out the shattered window and think, "I could die out there." Usually, it's more like the experience Gordon Snow describes in *Safe and Sound* (Goose Lane Editions): "You may have been feeling uneasy for some time, but you know for sure when you can't deny any longer that night will arrive before you do."

▶ What are four things you shouldn't do if you are lost?

Keep a bad situation from becoming worse by avoiding these common mistakes.

- Heading down an unknown trail, despite the fact that you don't know which way to go.
- Traveling off-trail with determination in a straight line figuring you'll get un-lost eventually.
- Walking downhill and/or downstream, even though you don't know where the stream or hill is headed.
- Hiking after dark. "Unless there is <u>imminent</u> threat to life or limb, any lost person is better off if they do not move," says Charley Shimanski, executive director, American Alpine Club and education director, Mountain Rescue Association.

TRAIN TO LIVE

A FAMOUS SURVIVOR SHARES
WHAT IT TAKES TO MAKE IT THROUGH

October 1993, Mogadishu, Somalia: Under heavy fire, Master Sergeant Tim Wilkinson, an Air Force pararescueman, ran back and forth several times between an <u>incapacitated</u> helicopter and a bullet-riddled building, carrying life-saving supplies and medical care to the wounded. He took bullets in his face and arm, and earned the Air Force Cross for extraordinary heroism. The movie *Black Hawk Down*

---

words for everyday use

im • mi • nent (i' mə nənt) *adj.,* ready to take place. *From the looks of the dark clouds, rain was imminent.*

in • ca • pac • i • tate (in kə pas' ə tāt) *v.,* disable. *I called a tow truck for my incapacitated car.*

immortalizes the unselfish acts of Wilkinson and his compatriots. "My training prepared me the best it could," he says. "You need to train for the type of environment you think you'll be facing, or else you'll have a false sense of security."

Wilkinson endured months of combat training to survive his ordeal; the backpacker's training regime is much simpler. Here are the easiest ways to train to survive a backcountry emergency[3]:

- Learn to swim, even if only at a beginner level.
- Take a first-aid class. Review it every three years.
- Exercise regularly. The stronger you are, the more hardship you can endure.
- Learn to navigate.
- Plan ahead. Brainstorm all potential disasters before you head out, and draft a plan for surviving each one.

◄ How can planning ahead help you?

CHEAT SHEET

THAT BITES. If a rattlesnake bites you and you're alone, walk out, say wilderness medical experts Robert Norris, M.D., and Sean Bush, M.D. Keep the bitten part as still as possible. Use a makeshift crutch for a bite on a lower extremity,[4] rest frequently, and drink often. Don't cut and suck. Don't use a tourniquet.[5] Don't ice it.

PANIC POISON. Stay calm. Your life depends on it. Stress produces cortisol, a hormone that circulates throughout your body for hours, interfering with

◄ What problems does panic often cause?

---

3. **backcountry emergency.** An emergency in a remote, rural, or undeveloped area
4. **extremity.** Hand or foot

---

words for everyday use

im • mor • tal • ize (im ôrt′ əl īz′) v., make immortal or famous. *The war heroes are immortalized in the statue in front of the state house.*
reg • ime (rā zhēm′) n., plan of action, especially for training purposes. *Twyla follows a strict regime of running and weightlifting to get in shape for playing basketball.*

en • dure (in dûr′) v., bear; suffer but live through. *I don't think I can endure another day of this heat.*
nav • i • gate (nav′ ə gāt′) v., find your way. *With some training you can learn to navigate by following the night stars.*

memory and ultimately wearing down axons and dendrites—critical parts in the region of the brain associated with memory. Experts say that panic is often <u>implicated</u> in disastrous survival decisions.

BEST SIGNALS FOR HELP. Use large rocks or tree limbs to spell "help," or draw an arrow to your shelter. Light three fires in a triangle—a universal distress signal. Use a flashlight, mirror (a CD works well), or other shiny surface to flash rescuers. Build a signal pole by hanging shiny or bright objects from a tree. Blow three long blasts on your emergency whistle or harmonica.

▶ What is the number one requirement for survival?

UNDER COVER. "Shelter is the number one requirement for survival. Water, fire, and food follow. If you're unable to make it back to your base camp, be prepared to build a shelter. A hut built out of forest debris will safely get you through the night." —*Tom Brown Jr., primitive skills expert and survival instructor for the U.S. military.*

Critical Thinking

1. According to Daryl Miller and Charles "Butch" Farabee, what traits do people need in a survival situation? Does Brian have these traits? Do you think you do? Explain.
2. Look at the four mistakes Farabee points out. Why do you think each of these could be a deadly mistake?
3. Review the list of ways to keep a bad situation from becoming worse. Summarize these tips in one sentence.
4. How might staying calm save your life?
5. What are the four requirements for survival? Which is first? Why? In *Hatchet,* how does Brian fulfill these requirements?

---

5. **tourniquet.** Device used to cut off blood flow to stop bleeding

words for everyday use

im • pli • cate (im' plə kāt) *v.,* bring into incriminating connection. *The suspect was implicated in the crime when his fingerprints were found at the scene.*

"skunk" and "mosquito"
by Valerie Worth

ABOUT THE RELATED READINGS

The following two poems, **"skunk"** and **"mosquito,"** look at two of the animals Brian encounters in *Hatchet*. In "skunk" and "mosquito," a speaker describes each animal's behavior.

Valerie Worth (1933–1994) wrote children's poetry and fiction for people young and old. In 1991, Worth received the Poetry Award for Excellence in Poetry for Children by the National Council of Teachers of English. The subject matter of Worth's poems were everyday objects, and she paid special attention to sound and rhythm.

"skunk"

▶ When is the poem set?

▶ What sense is most stimulated by lines 2–8?

▶ What does the skunk do?

Sometimes, around
Moonrise, a <u>wraith</u>
Drifts in through
The open window:
A <u>vague</u> cold <u>taint</u>
Of rank weeds
And phosphorescent[1]
Mold, a hint
Of <u>obscure</u> dank
Root hollows and
Mist-woven paths,
Pale toadstools and
Dark-reveling worms:
As the skunk walks
By, half vapor, half
Shade, <u>diffusing</u>
The night's <u>uncanny</u>
Essence and atmosphere.

---

1. **phosphorescent.** Giving off or displaying light caused by radiation

words for everyday use

wraith (rāth) n., ghost or gaseous form. *A wraith of smoke was all that was left of the house after the fire.*

vague (vāg) adj., not clearly felt or understood. *I had a vague sense of dread, but I couldn't say why.*

taint (tānt) n., smell of spoil. *Jody realized he had left the roast on the counter because the taint of rotting meat filled the air as soon as he opened the door.*

ob • scure (äb skyür´) adj., not clear, faint. *We tried to follow the obscure trail, but we kept finding ourselves uncertain about which way to turn next.*

dif • fuse (dif yüz´) v., scatter, distribute. *The smell started out strong in the kitchen, but it diffused as it made its way throughout the whole house.*

un • can • ny (un kan´ ē) adj., eerie, beyond normal. *It's almost uncanny the way Marcia seems to know what I'm thinking.*

"mosquito"

There is more
To a mosquito
Than her sting
Or the way she sings
In the ear:

◀ What two traits of the mosquito are mentioned in the first stanza?

There are her wings
As clear
As windows,
There are the sleek
Velvets on her back;

◀ What simile is used to describe the mosquito's wings?

She bends six
Slender knees,
And her eye, that
Sees the swatter,
Glitters.

◀ What does the mosquito see?

Critical Thinking

1. Based on the poems, what is the main characteristic of the skunk? the mosquito?
2. Compare and contrast the description of the mosquito in the poem with the description in Chapter 4 of *Hatchet*.
3. How do you think Brian would feel about the descriptions of the animals in these poems? Would he feel they were accurate? Why?
4. Choose one of these animals. What would you say about this animal?

Creative Writing Activities

Alternate Ending

What if Brian hadn't been rescued when he was? What do you think would have happened to him if he had had to survive in the forest in the winter? Write a chapter or two that tells what happens to Brian after he finds the survival pack. After you have written your story, you might want to read *Brian's Winter,* in which Gary Paulsen tells his version of Brian's story of wintering over in the wilderness.

News Story

Brian says there was a furor of media interest after the rescue. Imagine you are a reporter in one of these situations:
• You are writing for Brian's hometown newspaper
• You are writing for a national outdoors adventure magazine
• You are writing for a magazine about teen personalities
Write a feature story about Brian and his experience. Think about who your audience is. Choose details and a tone appropriate to your audience.

Journal Entries

Brian keeps a mental journal of his mistakes and of important events. Imagine Brian had paper and pen. Write journal entries about at least four important experiences. The experiences might be important firsts or lessons Brian learns.

Animal Poem

Brian notes that the animals he encounters often act little like the animals on nature shows on television. Choose an animal you have seen firsthand. It could be something big, like a bear, or something small, like a mosquito. Think about your own experience observing or encountering this wild animal. What did the animal look like? How did it sound?

How did it move? How did it affect you? How did you feel about it? Write a poem about the animal.

Description

Brian learns to observe his surroundings carefully. He notices the color and shape of things. He picks individual sounds out of background noise. He senses the presence of animals. Take some time observing a place. Look carefully at the place, even if you know it well. Close your eyes and listen to the sounds. Notice how the place smells and feels. Write a description of the place you choose. Include many sensory details in your description.

Based on Your Experience

Gary Paulsen wrote an autobiographical book called *Guts*. The book describes how Paulsen used his own experiences when writing *Hatchet* and other books about Brian. Think about an experience of your own that you could use in a story. It could be an adventure you had, a scary moment, a funny mistake, or an experience that many people share, such as moving to a new home. Write a story in which a character goes through the experience you chose. You can change the details of the experience as much or as little as you like.

Critical Writing Activities

Changing Character

Brian changes a great deal over the course of this novel. Write an essay that explores how he changes. Describe Brian at the beginning of the novel. Explain what experiences change him. Then assess whether this is a positive or negative change. You might begin by looking at the graphic organizers you completed about character while reading *Hatchet*.

Significant Setting

The setting of a novel is the time and place in which it takes place. Why is the setting of the novel important to the plot? How would the story have been different if Brian had crashed in a different place or different season? In a short essay, describe the setting and explain how the setting affects the plot.

Awards

Hatchet is a Newbery Honor Book. It has also won many other awards and honors. Why do you think this book has won so many awards? Imagine you were going to nominate *Hatchet* to the national list of top ten books for young people. Write an essay that nominates *Hatchet* for this honor. Give at least three reasons to explain why you think the book deserves to be honored.

Central Conflict

Brian's central conflict in *Hatchet* is surviving alone in the wilderness after the plane crash. Conflicts are often classified as external (a conflict with something outside the character) or internal (a conflict within the character). In order to survive, Brian has to face both internal and external conflicts. Write an essay explaining the conflicts Brian faces and how they affect his ability to survive.

Book Review

Write a book review of *Hatchet* or another book about Brian by Gary Paulsen. Other books about Brian include *Brian's Winter, Brian's Return, The River,* and *Brian's Hunt. Guts* is a nonfiction book in which Gary Paulsen describes the experiences he used when writing the Brian books. Your review should include a summary of the plot, though you may not want to give away the ending. Comment on why you think this book is or isn't a worthwhile read. You can tailor your review to be suitable for the newspaper, radio, television, or the Internet. You may want to present your review to the class or publish it on an Internet site.

Projects

Survival Guide

With a group of your classmates, create a survival guide. Choose one of the following scenarios or one of your own:

- You go hiking in the woods and get lost
- You are lost at sea
- You are injured on a snowy mountaintop
- Your vehicle breaks down in the dessert

Your survival guide should have two parts: how to prepare for possible dangers and what to do in case a problem arises. In the preparation section, include a list of things people should carry to be prepared.

Flora and Fauna Guide

Brian saw many animals and plants near the lake where he crashed in southeastern Canada. Some of those plants were good to eat, and some were useful for other reasons. Some of the animals were good to eat, and others were dangerous to him. With a group of your classmates, research the flora and fauna (or plants and animals) of southeastern Canada and create a guide that describes them. In your guide, provide pictures or details to help people identify the animal or plant. You may also want to include information for people trying to survive, such as what to do if they see a bear or whether or not a particular type of berry is good to eat. Alternatively, create a flora and fauna guide for the area in which you live.

Tornado Report

Just as Brian is getting things under control, a tornado sweeps through and upsets his shelter and supplies. Use the Internet and library resources to research tornadoes. Create a special report on tornadoes for your class. Include an oral report and visual aids, such as maps, posters, or a bulletin board. Answer the following questions and any questions of your own:

- How are tornadoes formed?
- How common are tornadoes in Canada? Where are they most common?
- How are tornadoes predicted?
- What should you do if a tornado strikes?
- What kind of damage can a tornado do?

Animals: Fact and Fiction

Brian realizes that the information people get about animals from nature shows, books, movies, and cartoons is not always accurate. With a group of your classmates, research one type of animal, such as a moose, bear, wolf, skunk, mosquito, or porcupine. Prepare a presentation or display that covers common misconceptions about the animal and important facts about the animal. Here are some of the questions you might try to answer:

- What characteristics do people usually think of when they think of this animal?
- What characters in books or movies might people associate with this animal?
- What does this animal eat?
- How does this animal protect or defend itself?
- How does this animal usually react to humans?

The Nature of Hope

Hope is very important to Brian's survival. This project gives you a chance to explore the importance of hope. First, take a poll of people in your school and community about what gives them hope and what they do when they are not feeling hopeful. Discuss with your classmates why hope is important. Then create an artistic work that demonstrates the power of hope. You can create a visual representation—a collage, a series of artworks or a bulletin board—or a performance piece—a song, an oral reading, a dance or a play.

Glossary of Words for Everyday Use

PRONUNCIATION KEY

VOWEL SOUNDS

		ō	go	ʉ	burn	
a	hat	ô	paw, born			
ā	play	u̇	book, put	ə	extra	
ä	star, father	ü	blue, stew		under	
e	then	oi	boy		civil	
ē	me	ou	wow		honor	
i	sit	u	up		bogus	
ī	my					

CONSONANT SOUNDS

b	but	l	lip	t	sit
ch	watch	m	money	th	with
d	do	n	on	th	the
f	fudge	ŋ	song, sink	v	valley
g	go	p	pop	w	work
h	hot	r	rod	y	yell
j	jump	s	see	z	pleasure
k	brick	sh	she		

abate (ə bāt') *v.*, decrease in intensity or amount.

ag • o • ny (ag' ə nē) *n.*, intense pain; distress.

as • set (as' et) *n.*, resource.

as • sume (ə süm') *v.*, take on.

au • di • ble (ôd' ə bəl) *adj.*, capable of being heard.

bat • ter (bat' ər) *v.*, hit repeatedly, beat.

bluff (bluf) *n.*, steep bank.

cav • i • ty (kav' ət ē) *n.*, hole or hollowed out space.

chip • per (chip' ər) *adj.*, happy and lighthearted.

con • sume (kən süm') *vi.*, use up, waste.

con • sum • ing (kən sü miŋ) *adj.*, engrossing, taking all attention.

con • vulse (kən vuls') *v.*, shake violently as with spasm.

cor • ro • sive (kə rō' siv) *adj.*, having the power to eat away.

crude (krüd) *n.*, rough.

de • press (di pres') *v.*, press down.

dif • fuse (dif yüz') *v.*, scatter, distribute.

di • min • ish (də min′ ish) *v.,* lessen.

dis • tort (di stôrt′) *v.,* twisted out of proportion or natural shape.

dor • mant (dôr′ mənt) *adj.,* asleep or inactive.

drone (drōn) *n.,* continuous deep buzzing or humming sound.

ed • dy (ed′ ē) *v.,* move like a whirlpool.

en • dure (in dúr′) *v.,* bear; suffer but live through.

ex • ten • sive (ik sten[t]′ siv) *adj.,* having a wide span or scope.

ex • ult (ig zult′) *v.,* rejoice.

flail (flā[ə]l) *v.,* beat or swing wildly.

fren • zied (fren′ zēd) *adj.,* marked by wild agitation or movement.

fu • ror (fyúr′ ôr) *n.,* craze; outburst of public excitement.

gin • ger • ly (jin′ jər lē) *adv.,* cautiously or carefully.

glis • ten (glis′ ən) *v.,* sparkle; give off a reflection like a polished surface.

grat • i • fy (grat′ ə fī) *v.,* satisfy, please.

gri • mace (grim′ əs) *v.,* to make a facial expression of disgust, disapproval, or pain.

heft (heft) *v.,* to lift or throw.

hok • ey (hō′ kē) *adj.,* corny.

horde (hôrd) *n.,* swarm, crowd.

hum • mock (hum′ ək) *n.,* small, rounded hill.

hur • tle (hʉrt′ əl) *v.,* move quickly with a rushing sound.

im • mi • nent (i′ mə nənt) *adj.,* ready to take place.

im • mor • tal • ize (im ôrt′ əl īz′) *v.,* make immortal or famous.

im • pli • cate (im′ plə kāt) *v.,* bring into incriminating connection.

in • ca • pac • i • tate (in kə pas′ ə tāt) *v.,* disable.

in • ces • sant (in ses′ ənt) *adj.,* continuing without interruption.

in • di • cate (in′ də kāt) *v.,* demonstrate or show by sign.

ini • tial (in ish′ əl) *adj.,* first.

in • ter • lace (int ər lās′) *v.,* connect by crossing or alternating.

in • ter • val (int′ ər vəl) *n.,* pause between events.

itin • er • ary (ī tin′ ə rer′ ē) *n.,* route or plan of a trip.

keen • ing (kēn′ iŋ) *adj.,* sharp; wailing.

lance (lan[t]s) *n.,* spear or other long, sharp object.

lev • i • tate (lev' ə tāt) *v.,* rise or float in the air.

loom • ing (lüm' iŋ) *adj.,* taking shape as an approaching object, often appearing larger than life or in distorted form.

lurch (lʉrch) *v.,* roll or tip suddenly.

mas • sive • ly (mas' iv lē) *adv.,* hugely; severely.

mi • nu • tiae (mi nü' shē ē') *n. pl.,* minor details.

mock (mäk) *v.,* mimic, imitate to make fun of.

mo • not • o • ny (mə nät' ən ē) *n.,* same to the point of being tedious.

mo • ti • vate (mōt' ə vāt) *v.,* provide with need or desire to act.

murky (mʉr' kē) *adj.,* dark and obscure.

nat • u • ral • ist (nach' rə ləst *or* nach' ər ə ləst) *adj.,* related to the study of natural history or field biology.

nav • i • gate (nav' ə gāt') *v.,* find your way.

ob • liv • i • ous (ə bliv' ē əs) *adj.,* unaware, without knowledge.

ob • scure (äb skyür') *adj.,* not clear, faint.

pain • stak • ing (pān' stā kiŋ) *adj.,* taking care and effort.

per • cep • ti • ble (pər sep' tə bəl) *adj.,* noticeable by the senses.

pre • vail • ing (pri vā' liŋ) *adj.,* most frequent or common.

pro • ce • dure (prə sē' jər) *n.,* series of steps for accomplishing something; usual way of doing something.

pros • pect (präs' pekt) *n.,* anticipation; possibility.

pul • ver • ize (pul' və rīz) *v.,* crush or grind into powder.

rank (raŋk) *adj.,* putrid, offensive in odor.

rasp • ing (rasp' iŋ) *adj.,* grating, irritating.

re • bel (ri bel') *v.,* oppose or resist.

re • cede (ri sēd') *v.,* move back or decrease.

re • gime (rā zhēm') *n.,* plan of action, especially for training purposes.

reg • u • late (reg' yə lāt) *v.,* control, order.

rel • a • tive (rel' ət iv) *adj.,* comparative.

re • ten • tion (ri ten' chən) *n.,* act of keeping or retaining.

rev • el (rev' əl) *v.,* take pleasure or satisfaction.

riv • u • let (riv′ yə lət) *n.*, small stream.

rue • ful • ly (rü′ fə lē) *adv.*, mournfully, regretfully.

scrawl (skrôl) *v.*, write quickly or carelessly.

sear (si[ə]r) *vi.*, burn or scorch.

sen • ti • nel (sent′ ə nəl) *n.*, guard.

slew (slü) *v.*, turn suddenly, skid.

slith • er • ing (slith′ ər iŋ) *n.*, sliding movement or sound.

spasm (spaz′ əm) *n.* sudden, involuntary muscle movement.

sty • mie (stī′ mē) *v.*, to stand in the way of.

sub • stan • tial (səb stan′ chəl) *adj.*, considerable in quantity.

taint (tānt) *n.*, smell of spoil.

tel • e • graph (tel′ ə graf) *v.*, to make known by signs in advance.

ten • dril (ten′ drəl) *n.*, slender bit that coils or curls.

trait (trāt) *n.*, distinguishing quality or characteristic.

trans • mis • sion (tran[t]s mish′ ən) *n.*, act of sending a message.

trem • ble (trem′ bəl) *v.*, shake involuntarily.

tur • bu • lence (tər′ byə lən[t]s) *n.*, violent, irregular motion or swirling agitation of water, air, or gas.

un • can • ny (un kan′ ē) *adj.*, eerie, beyond normal.

vague (vāg) *adj.*, not clearly felt or understood.

vul • ner • a • ble (vuln′ rə bəl *or* vul′ nə rə bəl) *adj.*, open to attack or damage.

wal • low (wäl′ ō) *v.*, roll lazily or act helpless.

wince (win[t]s) *v.*, to shrink or draw back slightly, usually with a grimace, as in pain, embarrassment, or alarm.

with • er (with′ ər) *v.*, shrivel and lose strength.

wraith (rāth) *n.*, ghost or gaseous form.

wrench (rench) *n.*, a sudden, sharp twist or pull.

Glossary of Literary Terms

CENTRAL CONFLICT. A **central conflict** is the main struggle between two people or things in a literary work. Conflicts in literary works are often human versus human, human versus nature, or human versus self. Brian experiences human versus nature and human versus self conflicts in *Hatchet*.

CHARACTER. A **character** is a person or animal who takes part in the action of a literary work. The action in *Hatchet* centers on thirteen-year-old Brian Robeson.

CHARACTERIZATION. **Characterization** is the act of creating or describing a character. Writers create characters using three major techniques: showing what characters say, do, or think; showing what other characters say or think about them; and by describing the physical features, dress, and personality of the character.

CLIMAX. The **climax** is the high point of interest or suspense in the plot of a story or play.

CRISIS. The **crisis**, or turning point, is the point in a plot when something happens to determine the future course of events and the eventual fate of the main character.

DÉNOUEMENT. In the plot of a story or play, the **dénouement** is any material that follows the resolution and that ties up loose ends.

DESCRIPTION. **Description** is a type of writing that portrays a character, object, or scene. Descriptions make use of *sensory details*—words and phrases that describe how things look, sound, smell, taste, or feel.

EXPOSITION. The **exposition** is the part of a plot that provides the background information, often about the characters, setting, or conflict.

FALLING ACTION. The **falling action** in a plot is all of the events that follow the climax.

FLASHBACK. A **flashback** is a part of a story, poem, or play that presents events that happened at an earlier time. Chapter 4 of *Hatchet* starts with a flashback.

INCITING INCIDENT. The **inciting incident** is the event that introduces the central conflict in the plot of a story or play. The inciting incident in *Hatchet* occurs in the first chapter.

MOTIVATION. A **motivation** is a force that moves a character to think, feel, or behave in a certain way.

PLOT. A **plot** is a series of events related to a central conflict, or struggle. A typical plot involves the introduction of a conflict, its development, and its eventual resolution. See pages 142–144 for a description of the elements of a plot and an analysis of the plot of *Hatchet*.

RESOLUTION. The **resolution** is the point in the plot of a story or play at which the central conflict is ended or resolved.

RISING ACTION. In the plot of a story or play, the **rising action**, or complication, develops the conflict to a high point of intensity.

SETTING. The setting is the time and place in which a literary work takes place. Most of *Hatchet* takes place in the summer near a lake in the Canadian wilderness.

Acknowledgments

ABCNews Internet Ventures. "Castaway Challenge: Teen Spends 48 Hours Alone on Island," August 28, 2001, by Thomas E. Goldstone. Courtesy of ABCNEWS.com. Reprinted with permission of ABCNews Internet Ventures.

Farrar, Straus and Giroux, LLC. "mosquito" and "skunk" (text only) from *all the small poems and fourteen more* by Valerie Worth. Copyright © 1987, 1994 by Valerie Worth. Reprinted by permission of Farrar, Straus and Giroux, LLC.

Lerner Publishing Group. "Walking on the Jornada del Muerto Desert" from *Finding Your Way: The Art of Natural Navigation* by Jennifer Owings Dewey. Text copyright © 2001 by Jennifer Owings Dewey. Used by permission of Millbrook Press, a division of Lerner Publishing Group. All rights reserved.

Rodale Press, Inc. "Survival: Be Prepared. Be Aware. Stay Alive" by Buck Tilton from *Backpacker* magazine, August 2002. Copyright © 2002 Rodale Press, Inc. Reprinted by permission of Rodale Press, Inc.

We have made every effort to trace the ownership of all copyrighted material and to secure permission from copyright holders. In the event of any question arising as to the use of any material, we will be pleased to make the necessary corrections in future printings. We are grateful to the authors, publishers, and agents listed here for permission to use the materials indicated.